Imm

RUBY
McCRACKEN

To Nathan and Simon, my co-authors

Kelpies is an imprint of Floris Books
First published in 2017 by Floris Books
Text © 2017 Elizabeth Ezra

This publisher acknowledges subsidy from
Creative Scotland towards the publication
of this volume

 Also available as an eBook

British Library CIP data available
ISBN 978-178250-446-7
Printed in Poland

RUBY McCRACKEN
TRAGIC WITHOUT MAGIC

ELIZABETH EZRA

Kelpies

CHAPTER 1

"Ruby, if you don't get up *this second* I'm throwing your spider eggs in the bin!"

I opened my eyes. I am *so* not a morning person. My mum always shouts a lot to get me out of bed, but I could tell she really meant business this time when she threatened to throw my breakfast away. Spider eggs are my favourite.

If I knew then what I know now, though, I would have closed my eyes and refused to get out of bed at all.

Dragging myself out from under my dragon-skin duvet, I washed and dressed quickly, wolfed down my spider eggs on toast, and knocked back a glass of bat milk. I picked up my backpack and Vronsky then bolted up the stairs into the attic. Vronsky's our family's familiar – a sleek black cat with bright gold eyes. He always comes to school with me – I'm pretty sure I'm his favourite family member. He likes to nestle in the bristles at the back of my broom while I dash around. Easy for some. Opening the hatch to the flyway, I grabbed my broom and leapt on. My take-off was a little hurried, and I nearly crashed into the tree in front of our house, I was going so fast.

"Hey, watch it – safety first!" Mum shouted out the window.

I checked to make sure the point on my hat hadn't got bent out of shape (I hate it when that happens), then flew off through the mist towards school.

We live on an island called Hexadonia. It's the biggest in a cluster of islands known as the Hexadonian Archipelago, and although all of the other school teams we played cockroach matches against said that their island was the best, they were *so* wrong.

I made it to the East Hexadonia Sorcery Academy with just a few seconds to spare. Mrs Zephyr, my class teacher, was tapping her fingers on the desk when I ran in, with Vronsky sauntering in behind me.

"Ruby McCracken," Mrs Zephyr said, in that voice I knew meant trouble.

"At your service," I said.

"You're late." The wart on the end of her large nose quivered.

I took out my pocket sundial. "No, I'm actually a few seconds early—"

"Don't talk back." She cut me off. "You're late if I say you're late. That'll be five minutes off your Shadow Time."

"But—"

"Would you like me to make it ten?"

"No," I mumbled, and trudged past the rows of wooden desks to my seat. Abigail and Margaret, my best friends, both gave me sympathetic eye rolls.

Losing Shadow Time meant that I would have to sit watching the others having fun at break without being allowed to join in. Shadow Time was the time in between lessons when we were allowed to do whatever we wanted for a few precious, non-boring minutes. I'd already lost five minutes on Monday for forgetting my homework, and another five on Tuesday for mislaying my reading jotter. I guess you could say I'm not so good at holding on to things.

We had a lesson that morning on history – the famously bloody Battle of the Hexadonian Archipelago. I tried to pay attention, especially during the gory bits, but my mind kept wandering. And besides, Vronsky was distracting me. Usually he dozes during my lessons (I can't blame him, some of them are *really* boring), but that day he kept nudging his nose into the palm of my hand to get me to stroke him. At the time, I thought he was just feeling affectionate, but of course now, looking back, I realise that he needed reassurance. It was as though he knew what was coming.

I didn't have cockroach practice after school, so I decided to make a quick getaway before Mrs Zephyr could find an excuse to dock any more Shadow Time. Grabbing my cape from the cloakroom, I unlocked my broom from the rack in front of the school, sat Vronsky on the back, and raced home.

The journey home was smoother than the ride to school had been, but as I approached my house, I saw something that made me stop suddenly in mid-air: my mum *and* my dad's brooms were both parked in the flyway. That was my first clue that all was not well. My parents never got home from work before 5.30 pm. Something was definitely off. Puzzled, I headed to the front door. We live – or rather, *lived* – in a big, three-storey house with turrets and cupolas and cobwebs everywhere. Nice and cosy. When I walked in, though, it didn't feel cosy. The whole family was sitting in the living room: my mum, dad and even my annoying little brother Carl. My parents both stood up as soon as I came in, as though they had been waiting for me.

"What are you doing home?" I asked, too confused by the weirdness of the situation to even say hello.

"Sit down, Slimeball," my dad said softly. He only ever uses affectionate names for me when he's feeling guilty about something, like the time he accidentally stepped on my pet toad, Norbert. Poor Norbert; he never hopped in a straight line again.

"What's happened?" I asked, more and more freaked out. It had to be something big for them to look so serious.

"Your father and I have something to tell you both," said my mum.

After a few moments, my father broke the tension. "We've lost our jobs."

There was a moment of shocked silence.

"What? *Both* of you?" I asked.

My mother nodded sadly, then came over to me and gently tweaked my nose. That sympathetic gesture said it all. I knew things must be really, *really* bad.

My parents both worked at ABC – the Aerozoom Broom Corporation. In fact, that's where they met, at an office party. My mum worked in public relations, and my dad was a manager in the product development department. They bonded over a shared love of slugrolls and toenail crisps at the buffet, and the rest is history. The Aerozoom Broom Corporation make brooms for all occasions – for sweeping and for flying (but mostly for flying). Their motto is 'One-stop shopping for all your household and aviation needs'.

"But what happened?" I asked.

"We were made redundant."

Carl piped in, "What does that mean?"

"It means they don't need us any more," my dad said.

"How can they not need you any more?" I said indignantly. "You're two of their best employees!"

Dad avoided my outraged gaze. "It is what it is. We can't change the situation now."

"There are just too many witches these days and not enough jobs," my mother sighed.

"Too many witches? How is that even possible?"

My dad said that with so many people in the Ordinary World getting fake witchery degrees off the internet and casting so-called 'spells', there was less work for the real witches. But this didn't make any sense to me. Wouldn't fake witches cast fake spells? And why would this affect real witches? And, anyway, wouldn't more witches boost broomstick sales, meaning that they'd need more employees, not fewer?

But as I started to question my dad's logic, he cut me off. "Look, it's complicated. But the long and short of it is that we no longer have jobs."

"But you can get new jobs, right?" said Carl, desperate to believe that everything would be OK.

My mum and dad exchanged glances. "Well, we *can* get new jobs. Just not... here."

I looked nervously at Carl.

"What do you mean *not here*?" I said slowly, as though drawing out my words would put off having to hear their answer.

"We're going to have to move," said Mum. "ABC is the only broom company in the Hexadonian Archipelago, and Hexadonia is the only one of the islands with a broom factory. If there are no jobs here, then..." She trailed off.

"We just can't afford to pay the magic bills any more," my dad added, as though that explained everything. "It's as simple as that."

Carl and I stared at them.

"I don't understand," I felt like there was more to this than my parents were letting on. "Why were you both fired at the same time?"

Dad stood up, as if he hadn't heard the question.

"Look, we have a lot to do to get ready for the move," said Mum. "We can talk about this later."

"But why do we have to leave *right away*?" I asked.

"You heard your mother," said Dad.

"But how—"

"That's ENOUGH," Dad bellowed, and I knew the conversation was over. My questions would have to wait. For now.

And that's how my life went from being just fine to being *awful*. Because not only did we have to move from Hexadonia, we had to move away from the Hexadonian Archipelago altogether, into the world of the Ords. The Ordinaries – the ridiculous, dopey, incomprehensible Ords.

I sometimes wish I could travel back in time to those innocent hours before I found out that my life was going to change for ever. If I could, I would savour every second – even when I was getting told off by Mrs Zephyr and could smell her morning toad juice on her putrid breath... Ah, happy memories. I guess it's easy to look back on the past with rose-tinted glasses. Now I live in the Ord World, I realise how great life was. I miss everything about living in Hexadonia, but these are some of the things I loved most:

Hexadonia Top 5

1. Flying to the top of the Jaggedy Peaks and then coasting all the way down on my broom with my hands in the air, howling into the wind.

2. Seeing the first snowfall in summer, when we'd throw snowcubes at each other during Shadow Time.

3. Playing in the school orchestra – my instrument was the pentangle.

   When we'd practised really, really hard we could all play out of tune at the same time.

4. Going with my mum to the Outdoor Insect Market, where I would help her buy juicy slugs and crunchy grasshoppers for dinner (and some centipedes for a treat to eat on the way home).

5. Watching The Hex Factor with my friends and chatting about who had been voted off, and who had been turned into toads.

But, as great as all those things were, the main reason I loved Hexadonia was quite simple:

It was my home.

After my parents broke the bad news to us, the big move happened surprisingly quickly. Over the next few days, we sold a lot of our belongings on wBay, and packed up everything else to take with us. I only went back to the Academy once, to say my goodbyes. The whole class had signed a card for me, and even Mrs Zephyr had a tear in her eye as she said farewell. Abigail and Margaret hugged me and told me to keep in touch. We crossed our wands and I vowed I would, but even as I said so I knew I probably wouldn't. Mum had told me that there was no way to communicate between our world and the Ord World. I tried not to think about that.

I also tried not to think about our cockroach team, the Sticky Witchets, for which I was the best bowler in my year group, if I do say so myself. In the changing room before my last practice, my teammates presented me with a snot-coloured tunic signed by everyone on the team. If I had stayed a minute longer, I would have dissolved into a blubbering mess of tears, so I took one last look around the room at all my friends, said goodbye, and ran out.

CHAPTER 2

The move was chaotic, to say the least. Even though we'd sold most of our belongings, we still had a lot of trunks and boxes to carry onto the boat and no one to help us. My dad kept telling us that boats almost never travel between the Hexadonian Archipelago and the Ord World, and that we had been lucky to find a cargo ship that was both passing our way and willing to take us, for a price. As we boarded the huge ship that would take us away from the life we had always known, it didn't feel lucky to me: It felt very, very unlucky.

It was still dark the morning we set off for the Ord World. Mum and Dad insisted that we board early, and they wouldn't even let stay me on the deck as we sailed away. They seemed kind of anxious for some reason; I guess moving is stressful. Before we went below deck, though, I took one last look at my island, Hexadonia. One last look at home. As I scanned the scenery, attempting to burn the image into my memory, I noticed three witches circling in the sky high above the port. We were the only islanders getting on this boat, and Mum and Dad had made us promise not to tell anyone which boat we were leaving on, so what were the witches looking for? Weird.

It was a nineteen-day journey on rough seas to the Ord World. Nineteen days at sea, couped up with my bludderfig of a brother, and made even worse by the fact that I was surrounded by water. I HATE water. Mum has to force me to take a shower once a week, during which I just scream. When we went to the seaside back home, I would wear a waterproof onesie at all times to protect myself from the water. When I was a toddler, my mum accidentally dropped me in the bath, and even though I was OK, it seems to have scarred me for life. Let's just say I'm never going to be a champion swimmer...

Life on the boat wasn't much fun. When I wasn't feeling seasick or trying to stop Vronsky from pouncing on sea gulls, I listened anxiously to the sound of waves lapping against the boat. Every day was the same: we would eat our rations of smoked snake brains and candied rat guts, using an overturned door as a dinner table; and I would ask my mum and dad why we had had to leave so suddenly. Their answer was always identical: "Stop asking so many questions, Ruby."

I tried to distract myself by imagining what our new life was going to be like, but that was actually pretty difficult, because I had no idea what to expect. When I first heard we were going to the Sceptered Isle I was intrigued, but my interest faded when I found out that this was another name for the United Kingdom.

I remembered studying a whole bunch of Ord countries at school, but all I knew about the UK was that they had a queen (so why wasn't it called the United Queendom, I wondered?), and they had a lot of tanning salons.

Then my dad explained that, within the United Kingdom, we were going to a place called Scotland. I did some research and found out that they liked to eat a food there made out of sheep intestines, so maybe it wouldn't be so bad.

Hauling most of your worldly possessions onto a boat and setting sail for a foreign land isn't something you do every day. But even though I was sad to leave my home behind, I was actually pretty relieved when we dropped anchor in the bustling port of a city called 'Edinburgh'. Mostly just because I would be on dry land again. The minute we stepped off the boat, however, I noticed that something didn't feel quite right. For one thing, my parents kept glancing around anxiously, almost as though they were looking for someone. I didn't know who they thought they might see, because we definitely didn't know anyone here. But I felt different, too – like something was missing, but I didn't know what.

I wondered if I was feeling weird because I hadn't eaten anything in a while. "I'm hungry," I told my mum. "I need a snack."

"No, wait—" she said, but it was too late. I mouthed the Snack Spell:

Eye of newt and hoof of yak,
Let's conjure up a tasty snack.

Nothing happened.

I frowned. How could I get the Snack Spell wrong? It's practically the first spell a witch learns. *I must really be tired*, I thought, and, before my mum could stop me, I tried again.

Still, nothing. Zero. Zilch.

Carl giggled. He loves to see me mess up.

I looked at my mum in panic.

She shook her head. "Our magic stopped working when we left Hexadonia."

"Wait a minute," I said. "You and Dad are the ones who lost your jobs. How come *my* magic doesn't work either?"

"We were on a family plan," said Dad.

"So you mean—"

"'Fraid so," said Mum.

"You mean *my* magic doesn't work either?" Carl screeched; apparently the reality of the situation had taken a minute or two longer to reach his tiny, pinhead brain.

Now I was the one giggling. "Guess you won't be able to make your delicious magic mud pies any more," I said with mock sadness. Everyone knew that Carl's magic mud pies were a disaster. They tasted like chocolate – absolutely disgusting.

"Shut up!" Carl shouted.

"That's enough from both of you!" my dad scolded. But his heart wasn't in it. He seemed distracted, and kept looking around. I hoped we weren't lost already. That would be a great start to our new life.

We had just begun walking up a long ramp when I noticed that my mother was wearing a fur coat. Well, more of a wrap, really, which I'd never seen before. Dad had made it clear we needed to travel light, so why had she bought new clothes? I had read that the UK can be cold in October, but it wasn't *that* cold. I opened my mouth to speak, but the way my dad glared at me made it clear this wasn't the time for another question.

The long ramp we seemed to have been walking on forever led us to a big, white concrete building. It looked very official.

"Where are we going?" I asked Mum

"We have to go through passport control."

"Oh," I said, as though I understood, but her reply raised more questions than it answered. Didn't you need *passports* to go through passport control? I couldn't remember ever getting a passport, let alone having brought them with us. We'd never left the Hexadonian Archipelago before.

We walked into a large room filled with people waiting in long queues that zigzagged back and forth like snakes. Yum, *snake*. My stomach grumbled loudly.

We joined a queue, pushing our enormous pile of

luggage in front of us, and copied everyone else (taking tiny little steps forward while tutting), until it was finally our turn to approach the kiosk.

"Passports," the official behind the desk said in a bored voice.

My dad took four bright purple booklets embossed with gold lettering from his coat pocket and laid them in front of the man, who picked them up and began idly leafing through them. Suddenly he stopped and, wide-eyed, looked up at my parents.

"Your majesties," he said in a hushed tone and took off his hat, smoothing down his curly hair.

"Hey, why's he calling you—" I began, but my mother – my own mother! – stepped on my foot hard with her heeled bat-skin boots. "Ow!" I yelped.

"It's an honour to have you in our country," the official continued. He had been slouching, but now he sat up straight. "May I ask what brings you to our fair land?"

My parents looked at each other. They both spoke at once.

"Holiday," said my mother.

"Classified business," said my father.

"A classified business holiday?" said the official, scratching his head.

"That's right – a classified business holiday." My mother nodded.

"Ah," said the official, still looking perplexed.

"Yes, that's why we've brought the children," said Dad.

"For the holiday part, not the classified business part," he added.

"Ah." The official seemed happy with that response. Then something appeared to occur to him. "May I ask what *kind* of classified business?"

"It wouldn't be classified any more if we told you," my dad said apologetically.

"Yes, of course." The official nodded quickly.

"Well, thank you for the very kind welcome." My mother had a huge smile plastered across her face. "If the rest of the Scottish people are as welcoming as you are, then we're going to have a wonderful stay."

The customs official blushed and stamped all four passports. "Thank *you* for taking the time to visit our country. I hope you enjoy your... classified business holiday," he said, pleased that he had remembered.

We were ushered through a set of automatic doors, and immediately came upon yet another queue. They really seemed to like standing in lines here. At the front, people were hefting their luggage onto a big conveyor belt, which carried it through a machine that showed everything inside. A bit like a Transparency Spell. A notice on the side said 'X-ray'.

I took the opportunity to dig for more info. "Dad, where did you get those passports? And why did the man call you 'your majesty'? We're not royalty."

"Shhhh!" my parent both hissed in unison.

"But what's—"

"Be *quiet*," my mother whispered. "We'll talk about this later!"

I didn't dare say anything more. When it was our turn with the X-ray machine, we lifted our bags onto the conveyor belt. A large woman with ginger hair and cat's-eye glasses sat slumped behind a monitor, chewing on the end of a biro. She wore a nametag on her jacket that said

As our suitcases disappeared into the tunnel, Mabel suddenly sat up. She stared intently at the screen. I could see what she was looking at from where I was standing: in my mum's suitcase, nestled in among the clothes and shoes, was the outline of a large, pointy, triangular object. They'd obviously found her hat. I wondered what they'd make of our cauldron and collapsible broomsticks. Mabel motioned to her colleague, a small man with a bowl haircut and a moustache, who approached the monitor. After the two of them consulted for a moment, the man said, "I'm going to need you to open this suitcase, Madam."

My mother's face paled. She adjusted her fur wrap, and was just about to say something when the customs official who had stamped our passports came running into the room. He tipped his hat at us then whispered something in Mabel's ear. She immediately stood up and saluted my parents.

"Your majesties," she said.

"I'm so sorry about this," the customs official said quickly. "Please accept our sincere apologies."

"No worries," said Dad.

Mabel curtsied repeatedly and bowed her head. "We wish you a pleasant trip in bonny Scotland."

"Thank you so very much," my mother said with a regal smile, almost as if she was enjoying herself. "We'll be sure to send you an autographed royal photo." And with that, she picked up her trunk, nodded to the rest of us to take ours, and breezed out of the room as we followed behind her.

CHAPTER 3

When we got outside, I was so confused by what had just happened that I almost didn't notice our surroundings. Apparently we were in the beautiful and historic capital city of Scotland. The skies were grey, the buildings were grey, and, by the look of it, the people were grey, too.

As soon as we were on our own I asked, "What was that all about? Since when are we royalty?"

"We're not," Dad said. "We just didn't want any hassles at passport control."

"But how did—"

"Before we left, we used most of our remaining magic to conjure up these special passports. It just makes things easier here."

"Huh. OK." I looked over at Carl who didn't seem to have noticed our new royal status. Ah, the ignorance of youth.

We shoved our luggage into a taxi waiting outside the building (not a broom taxi, I might add, but a boring old Earth-bound vehicle). It seemed like we had brought a lot of stuff as the driver heaved and squeezed everything into the car, yet I couldn't believe that this was all that remained of our old life. I felt like crying, but I didn't. Carl would never have let me live it down.

Suddenly I had a thought. "Where's Vronsky?" I looked around us in a panic. He had been with us on the boat, but I couldn't see him anywhere now.

"Don't worry, he's right here!" Mum said.

I stared at her blankly as she held out her empty arms. She looked like a magician who had just made someone disappear.

"Right *where*?" I was starting to worry that the stress of losing her job and spending nineteen days at sea had caused her to go a bit... peculiar.

"Here!" she said again. I still couldn't see anything, but then I noticed that the fur wrap around Mum's shoulders was beginning to unfurl slowly, before jumping down onto the ground in a clumsy heap. It wasn't a wrap at all – it was a rather large black dog.

"What's that?" I screeched.

"Oh, Slimeball," Mum said gently. "We didn't know how to tell you..." She gestured towards the dog.

"What? Why is this dog here? And where's Vronsky?" I looked blankly from my mum to my dad. Then, after a long minute, it dawned on me.

"No. Surely not. This creature... this creature is *Vronsky*?"

The dog flicked its tail slowly and began to purr as it tried to wrap itself (unsuccessfully) around my legs.

"It's a real hassle bringing animals into this country,

so I got him to hop on my shoulders for a little nap as we left the boat. I think he makes a very convincing wrap, don't you?"

"I don't care that you've been wearing him round your neck! *Why* and *how* did he turn into a dog?"

"Well, I suspected this might happen. The air here is different, and it can do strange things to familiars. They're magical creatures, after all."

I was about to point out the contradiction of having a strange familiar, when my mum spoke again.

"Be gentle with him," she said. "He doesn't understand what's happened. He still thinks he's a cat."

The taxi pulled up to a small pebbledash bungalow on a street filled with other small pebbledash bungalows. You had to look carefully to tell them apart.

"Is this our new house?" I gasped.

My mum nodded grimly. "I'm afraid so."

"But, but—" I stuttered. "It looks so... *ordinary*."

My mum shrugged. "Well, this *is* the Ordinary World. I guess the Ords like this sort of thing."

"Where are the turrets?" Carl asked. "Where are the cobwebs? And WHERE'S THE FLYWAY?" He pressed his face up against the car window, panicked.

But before anyone could reply, the driver cut in. "That'll be £14.90, love."

"Keep the change," my mum said, handing him four bronze ingots.

The driver gave her an odd look. "Very funny," he said, but he wasn't laughing. "Like I said, that'll be £14.90."

My father intervened. "Is there a problem?"

"*Is there a problem?*" the driver repeated incredulously. "The fare is £14.90. Pay up." He handed back the ingots.

"Uh-oh," Mum muttered, "we forgot to convert the cash."

"Will this not do?" Dad asked. "It's bronze."

"Look, pal. It's £14.90 in *real* money, or I'm callin the police. Stop messin about."

It was then that Vronsky decided to chip in. He hissed and arched his back. The driver eyed up Vronsky, then my mum, and my dad, and then looked back at Vronsky. Before I could stop him, Vronsky leaped out of his seat and across the taxi, extending one paw like a canine kung-fu warrior. He slammed into the driver with a heavy thud and clung on tight.

The driver let out a terrified howl.

The sleeve of his jumper was ripped just below the shoulder. "What *is* that thing?" he shouted.

"It's a cat, obviously," said Carl.

26

"Dog," I corrected.

"Cat," Carl insisted.

"Dog," I said again.

Vronsky was now crouching in the passenger seat of the taxi, next to the driver. He hissed again menacingly. I was impressed; Vronksy's usually pretty laid-back.

The driver immediately jumped out of the taxi, ran round to the side where my dad was sitting and began to pull the trunks out, dumping them in the street. "Get out of my cab – now!" he shouted.

"Your money—" Mum started to say, but he hopped back into the taxi and pulled away, careening round the corner so fast that his tires made a screeching sound.

"Well, that was... interesting." Mum took a large folded umbrella out of her trunk. It wasn't raining, so I could only guess that my earlier theory about the journey being a bit too much for her was actually correct, and that she was cracking up before my eyes.

As we walked up to the door of the house, I suddenly had a thought. "If we don't have any Ordinary money, how will we pay for everything?"

"We converted our remaining ingots into pounds to pay the first month's rent and to have a little in the bank for emergencies," Dad said, "but we forgot to convert the small amount of cash we brought. Your mother and I will have to get jobs right away to put food on the table and pay next month's rent."

"We don't have any cash?" I said weakly, trying

(without much success) not to panic. "What are we going to do for food until you find work?"

My mum thrust her spiky umbrella into the air just as a fat pigeon was passing. "Voilà," she said. "Roast pigeon, anyone?"

CHAPTER 4

"Ruby, if you don't get up *this second* I'm throwing your eggs in the bin!"

I opened my eyes. Nope; still not a morning person. I hadn't slept very well for thinking about today. We had been in the Ord World for a few days, but this was my first day at my new school. I was dreading how different Ord school was going to be. Plus, I wouldn't know anyone. I'd be a complete loner.

I picked at my breakfast, if you can call it that – they eat eggs from *chickens* here, blecch! – and pulled on my uncomfortable new school clothes. The uniform looked like something Vronksy would have dragged in back when he was a cat. Firstly, it's *green and gold* – whatever happened to good old black? There's also something called a blazer, which piqued my interest when I first heard of it because I thought it might occasionally burst into flames, but it just turned out to be a boring jacket.

The oddest thing about the uniform, though, is that there's no hat. I couldn't believe it when I found out. No hat? What's that about? I would feel positively naked without a hat. So at the weekend, I found a shop that sold hats and convinced my mum that this qualified as an emergency so she would take a little money out of our rapidly dwindling bank account. The shop I found was actually a ski shop, and the hat I got is a fleece snow hat, but it's better than nothing.

As I wrestled with my tie, Vronksy looked at me sadly from the bed. I sank down next to him. "Sorry, Vronsk, familiars aren't allowed in Ord school." He whined and nudged my hand. "I know, but wish me luck." He flicked his tail as I took one last look at myself in the mirror and sighed. "I think I'm going to need it."

"Bye, Mum!" I shouted as I ran up the stairs into the attic and climbed through a hatch in the ceiling onto the roof. Carl was already up there, grinning his annoying little face off.

"Why do *you* look so happy?" I asked as I fastened the clasp on my cloak and did my pre-flight checks.

"No reason," he smirked. I noticed he was holding an old camcorder he'd found in the house.

"Where did you get that from?" I asked. "Are you filming my amazing technique to get some tips?"

"Something like that," he said, smirking. Ugh, little brothers. I didn't have time to wonder what he might be up to now; I had to go.

"Whatever, I'm late!" I yelled. "Watch and learn, pinhead!"

I hopped onto my broom, took a short run-up and leapt into the air. It was only when I'd launched myself off the roof that I remembered.

You need *magic* to fly.

Fortunately, I landed in the hedge. I say fortunately. The branches shredded my skirt and scratched my skin, and my broom smashed on the hard ground of the driveway. Today was not going to be a good day.

I heard Carl's gleeful laughter from above.

"YOU'RE DEAD!" I screamed up at him. "You let me jump off the roof just so you could get a funny video! I could have died!"

"This is gonna go viral," he hollered happily and disappeared from view. Unfortunately, I was going to have to wait until after school to kill him. I couldn't be late on my first day.

OK, so guess how the Ords get to school. By broom? Nah – that would make too much sense. By magic carpet? Nope; guess again. Teleportation, you say? Wrong, wrong, wrong. They go on *foot*. Some of them have their parents drive them if they live far away, or they catch a strange long Ord vehicle called a 'bus'. But most of them actually walk on their own two feet. Weird.

It takes them forever to get to school, like fifteen or twenty minutes sometimes. And to cross the road, instead of air traffic controllers, they use lollipop ladies. (When I first heard this, I pictured a giant creature with a perfectly round, brightly coloured head and a long, spindly body; the reality turned out to be so much less interesting. It's just like the Ords to take an intriguing idea and turn it into something boring.)

Then, when they get to school, Ord pupils have to line up in front of their classroom door until a teacher lets them in – where's the fun in that? No flying around the playground trying to knock each other off brooms like at my old academy.

Sighing, I started walking. Unfortunately, Carl and I would be going to the same school. My dad had shown me the way the day we arrived, and made me practise the route until I knew it by heart. He was planning to walk with Carl and wasn't happy about me making my own way there, but I'm twelve, after all (well, twelve in Ord years; I'm actually 497). And there was no way I was going within sight of my gargoyle of a brother now, not after what he'd done.

As I walked to school, I thought about my friends back home, and the landscape, and even the Academy – and how different everything is here. I missed Abigail and Margaret. I missed smashing a rival cockroach team with the Sticky Witchets. I missed home. I knew I would have to get used to Ord life, but why couldn't I have at least been allowed to keep my magic? My life was so unfair, it was actually tragic.

When I got to school, which was in a hideous modern two-storey building with no turrets and hardly any cobwebs, I reported to the office, and the head teacher –

a short, plump woman with curly brown hair and dangly earrings called Mrs Dornan – insisted on taking me into the classroom herself to introduce me to the other pupils. So, so mortifying.

"Boys and girls," she began. "I'd like you to welcome a new pupil, Ruby McCracken."

"Hello Ruby," the class intoned. I scanned the room. I don't know what I was looking for; maybe a sympathetic face, or at the very least, someone who looked vaguely interesting. But all I saw was a sea of sameness: some pupils were big and some were small, some were girls and some were boys, some had yellow hair and some had black hair, but all of them, every single one, had that blank Ord look. In other words, a total absence of magic.

It was going to be a long year.

"Ruby, this is your teacher, Ms MacLean." She gestured to a younger woman with short blonde hair and horn-rimmed glasses.

I held out my hand for Ms MacLean to kiss (the standard Hexadonian custom when greeting a stranger), and she paused for a moment, then took it awkwardly and shook it.

"Pleased to meet you, Ruby." She looked at my nervous face and shredded skirt and smiled encouragingly.

I nodded. "Charmed, I'm sure." That was my little joke – but of course, the teacher didn't get it.

Ms MacLean bent down and spoke in my ear. "Can I ask you to take your hat off, please?" she whispered. "We don't wear them in the classroom."

No hats in the classroom? I suddenly panicked.

"Uh, I need to wear it because of my... because of my disease!" I said triumphantly, relieved I had come up with something.

Ms MacLean looked flustered. "Your *disease*? Oh. Is it infectious?" She recoiled, sidling away from me. "Nevermind," she mumbled quickly, as if she didn't want to hear any gross details, "if you need to wear it, that's fine."

Casting a dubious glance at my hat, she stood up and spoke loudly so the whole class could hear. "So where are you coming to us from, Ruby?"

"I come from..." I stopped, I wasn't sure what to say. Our parents had asked us not to tell anyone about our *situation*. "I come from an island," I said finally, which is the only thing I could think of, because it was true.

Ms M smiled broadly. "How wonderful! Arran? Skye?"

I swallowed and shook my head. Everyone was looking at me. And not in an oh-isn't-our-new-classmate-cool-and-interesting kind of way.

"Orkney?" Ms M prompted.

"No... further north," I stammered.

"Shetland?"

"Beyond Shetland."

"Hmm. Beyond Shetland. I guess I'm out of ideas."

There was a silence. Ms M seemed to be waiting for me to say something. "So, where *are* you from?" she said at last.

"I am a... citizen of the world," I said. Which was also true; I just didn't specify *which* world.

Ms M nodded and said approvingly, "As are we all, dear. As are we all." She waved goodbye to Mrs Dornan, who was already heading out the door, then pointed to an empty desk. "Take a seat in the third row, Ruby, and let me know if you have any questions."

"I do, actually," I said, looking around at the flimsy plastic tables and chairs. "Where are the inkwells?"

Ms M blinked. "The what?"

"The inkwells," I repeated. "You know – for dipping quills in." I drew my lucky quill from its silver sheath to show her.

"No quills, I'm afraid," Ms M said. "Just regular pens and pencils. The usual," she added, a bit warily, I thought.

"Oh. OK," I said calmly, even though a voice in my head was screaming, *What? No inkwells? These people are savages!* I walked quietly to my desk and could feel twenty-eight pairs of eyes boring into me as I took my seat. I made a mental note to bring some invisibility potion to school the next day.

But then I remembered – I didn't have any. Without magic to make them work, we had had to sell all of our invisibility potions and transformation potions on wBay. I would just have to put up with being gawked at for a while. Brilliant.

Ms M returned to the lesson she had been teaching when I came in. Something about geometry. "Now class," she turned to the white board, "who can tell me what kind of angles there are?"

"A broken angle!" someone shouted from the back of the room, to the sound of laughter.

"Very funny, Timothy," the teacher said, but she didn't seem to find the comment funny at all. She looked at the rest of the class expectantly.

"A right angle?" someone said hesitantly.

"Very good, David," said Ms M. "Anyone else?"

I raised my hand.

"Yes, Ruby," she said brightly.

"A pentangle."

"A pentangle?"

"A pentangle. A five-pointed star made from five intersecting straight lines. Also known as a pentagram or, if it has a circle around it, a pentacle. It's commonly used as a symbol for witchcraft."

Ms MacLean looked at me quizzically. "You... you certainly know a lot about angles," she said finally.

"Not really. Just pentacles," I said honestly.

Funnily enough, even though I often put my hand up to answer questions, Ms M didn't call on me again that day.

CHAPTER 5

As bad as the morning was, lunchtime was even worse. There are just as many cliques here as there were back at my old school, but at least I was near the top of the pecking order there. Here, I'm at the bottom – the lowest of the low.

The minute I walked into the canteen, my senses were assaulted by a combination of horrible smells. Following my nose to the source of the odour, I saw a counter laden with unbelievably disgusting piles of steaming tripe. Actually, real tripe would have been a treat compared to this stuff. There were unspeakable things involving potatoes, and big round discs with cheese on top and a red sauce (which initially looked interesting, until I realised it wasn't actually blood). The last option was a mysterious item called 'lasagne', which looked like something a cat had vomited up, so I chose that. It came with a tiny portion of salad, but at least it was wilted, so that was OK.

I carried my tray into the dining area, which was heaving with people talking and shouting and laughing.

Stopping at the first empty seat I could find, I dumped my tray of unappetising mush down on the table. Several boys who were eating next to me whispered to each other, and then got up to leave.

I looked down at my food and pushed it around the plate with my fork. My head was roasting inside my fleece hat, but I would have felt exposed without it so I kept it on.

Suddenly the entire room fell quiet – from a loud din to absolute silence in a tenth of a second. You could have heard a dead mouse squeak.

And then I saw why. Three girls came swaggering into the canteen. They were in school uniform, but everything else they wore was purple. Purple nail varnish, purple ribbons and hair clips, purple watches, purple backpacks, purple shoes. One of the girls was clearly the leader. She was tall, with long blonde hair, and she swept past all the other kids like a queen before her green and gold subjects. Her two purple minions followed her obediently. Every eyeball in the room was trained on them.

To my horror I saw the trio heading towards my table. Averting my eyes, I suddenly found something very interesting to stare at on my plate. The three Purple Girls stopped in front of me. Purple Girl Number Two, who was short and slim, also with blonde hair, said something to Number Three, who was taller and dark-haired. Number Three laughed.

"Ahem..." The leader did that fake throat-clearing thing you do when you want to get someone's attention.

"Yes?" I mumbled, looking up.

"I'm Georgia Finnegan." She smiled. "And you are...?"

"Ruby."

"Pleased to meet you, Ruby. This is Kirsty, and this is Rachel." She paused. "And these are our seats."

OK, I should have just let them have their stupid seats, but I was stressed and grouchy from my first day at school. "What do you mean, *your* seats?" I said.

"I mean, *our* seats." Georgia's smile grew even wider. "Isn't that right, Kirsty?" There was something a bit theatrical about the way she spoke, as though she were rehearsing lines for the world's worst play.

Kirsty, the short one, giggled. "Yes, that's right."

"So, move," said Georgia.

Right then, I should have moved. But I didn't really understand. "Th-th-these are the school's seats! They're not yours," I stuttered.

Georgia's eyes narrowed, and she suddenly resembled a horn-tailed serpent about to devour a field mouse. "Look, you weird ski-hat wearing loser, clearly you don't know who I am." She glanced up at the fifty-odd kids watching us, and her manner suddenly changed. "These are our seats, aren't they?" she said innocently. "If any of you think otherwise, please let me know," she added in a voice dripping with honey. No one said a word.

"See?" Georgia turned back to me, snarling again. "So move."

There was no point in arguing further, so I got up and walked to a different table, where I sat all by myself.

Conversations gradually resumed. I looked over at the Purple Mafia. They were whispering, giggling and pointing at me. The chair I had been sitting in was still empty, as though they couldn't stand to sit where I'd been.

I felt tears sting my eyes, but I wouldn't let them see me cry. This was all a total nightmare. One day I'm a happy-go-lucky young witch without a care in the world, and then before I know it I'm trapped in this unimaginable place where I don't know how anything works, with a bunch of creatures I don't understand, who seem to enjoy being mean to me.

Why did *both* my parents have to lose their jobs at the same time? And why did they drag me to this horrible place?

The rest of the day went by in a blur. I couldn't pay attention to my afternoon lessons because I was so upset about the incident in the canteen. When the bell rang for hometime, I nearly flew out of the classroom – nearly, but sadly, I didn't *actually* fly. I collected my cape from the cloakroom and walked out the school gate, remembering wistfully what it felt like to fly through the air with the wind in my hair and the countryside stretched out like a jigsaw far below. Lost in my daydreams, I nearly tripped over a furry object that pressed itself against my leg. I looked down to see a large black dog, forgetting for a second that it was Vronsky. His tail, which moved slowly from side to side, formed a long 'S' shape around my legs.

"Hey there, V." I was really glad to see a familiar face. Well, actually really glad to see my familiar. "Have you come to walk me home?"

Vronsky said nothing, of course, but nuzzled me and made a snuffling noise that sounded like a canine version of purring. I took this to be a 'yes'.

As I walked, and Vronsky sauntered, down the street, I noticed other school children whispering and giggling. I gave them the closest equivalent of the Evil Eye that I could manage under the circumstances – i.e. Not Having Magic. If we were back home these cretins would all be covered in pus-filled boils by now. Some people stopped laughing and looked a little nervous, but others just sniggered harder. I decided to ignore them and focus on my surroundings. The school was situated on a cobblestone street next to a small park. If I looked in the other direction, I could see Arthur's Seat – a big green hill rising up in the distance.

Because my dad had made me practise walking to school so many times, I'd got to know the neighbourhood pretty well. The small park across from school was called the Links, which was surrounded by blocks of flats. Nothing was more than a few hundred years old here. Back on Hexadonia, if your house was less than ten thousand years old it was considered brand new. Even Edinburgh Castle only dates from about 1100 AD; personally, I'm not that keen on modern architecture, but Ordinary people seem to like it.

Vronsky and I made our way towards the park, and I

noticed a couple of people kicking a ball around on the grass. As we grew closer, I saw that the 'people' were in fact my dad and brother, and the 'ball' they were kicking around was actually a skull.

"Hi," I said as I got nearer. "Have you been hanging around here since you picked up Carl?" Even though we go to the same school, Carl gets out half an hour before me because he's in one of the lower year groups.

"Yeah, thought we'd wait for you, seeing as it's your first day." My dad expertly brought the skull to a halt beneath his foot; he'd been a pretty good skullballer back in the day, and still had his Warlocks United strip, with an ad for Brunhilda's Brew on the back. I have to say that I've never seen the point of skullball. Give me a good game of cockroach any day.

My dad came over and tweaked my nose. I was a little embarrassed to be seen engaging in such mushy displays of affection in public, but I was also really glad to see him after the horrible day I'd had. I was just about to tell him what Carl had done to me that morning, when I heard a voice coming from the ground.

"Nice one."

I looked down to see a skull, which was yellowed with age. We'd brought it on the boat when we'd heard that sports shops in Scotland don't sell skulls.

"I see you've been working on your cranium control," the skull continued. "but it's still a far cry from the good old days, eh mate?"

My dad glowered at the skull. "Thanks a lot, Jeremy. "

"Just saying," the skull said.

"Well, don't," was my father's reply.

"Ooh, *someone* got up on the wrong side of the coffin this morning," the skull taunted.

My dad rolled his eyes. "Anyway, Slimeball," he turned to me. "how was your day?"

"Don't want to talk about it," I muttered.

"My day was great," Carl chimed in.

"Nobody asked you," I growled.

"Ah ah ah," my dad said, by way of warning.

"Well, *I'm* asking me," Carl said. "And my day was great, thank you very much. My teacher's pretty cool. She's a goth. She wears black and has a piercing in her lip."

"You have all the luck," I said.

"What's your teacher like?" Dad asked me.

"She's OK. Nothing wrong with her as far as I can tell, but it's early days."

"That's good."

"It's the kids who are horrible."

My dad raised his eyebrows. "Why, what did they do?"

I shook my head and kicked at a tuft of grass. "I don't want to talk about it, Dad."

He looked like he was about to say something, and then stopped himself. "Well, if you ever do, just say the word."

I nodded.

My dad scrutinised his watch. He had bought a cheap Ord one soon after we arrived here, and he was still getting used to it. "It's nearly... four o'clock. We should get going. I'm sure you both have homework, and we wouldn't want you to get off on the wrong footing."

"Speaking of footing," said a voice from the ground.

Carl kicked Jeremy up into his hands and stuffed him in his backpack. There was a muffled scream.

"What a drama queen." Dad shook his head.

Dad and Carl began to walk up ahead, engrossed in a boring conversation about skullball. I was just stopping Vronsky from pouncing on an unsuspecting pigeon when I noticed three cyclists wheeling slowly past in a line. Peering back at us, their bikes wobbled dangerously as they pedalled. They were all women, not quite old but getting there, and they were dressed in bulky cardigans and voluminous tracksuit bottoms. Instead of helmets, each wore a massive woolly hat, and I do mean *massive*. The last one in the line, who wore a pair of cracked gold-rimmed spectacles, must have fallen off at some point too, because she had a crooked wheel and bits of twigs and grass sticking out of her hat at funny angles.

Why were they staring at us? Maybe they were just tourists who were lost. Ords are so weird. I was going to point them out to my dad, but when I turned to look at them again, they were gone.

CHAPTER 6

Later that week, I was moping around the house after school, bored out of my mind and wishing like crazy that I had my magic back, when suddenly I had a thought. Where's the first place you look if you're trying to find something? Where do you begin every search? The internet, of course! Why didn't I think of this sooner?

The day after we moved here, my dad found an old computer up in the attic which must have been left here by the previous tenants. He dusted it off, plugged it in, and we were all surprised to see that it still worked. So when no one was in the living room, I sat down at the computer to try my luck.

They have something called Google here, which is a lot like Woogle, except it only works in two dimensions. Still, it was worth a shot.

I typed in 'how to get magic', figuring that I'd have to try lots of different wordings, but a website popped up on the screen straight away. It said:

Are you tired of waiting for the magic to happen?

You could say that, I thought.

Would you like a 100% guaranteed way to get magic?

Sure, I thought. That sounds great.

Would you like your magic to be absolutely free, with no questions asked and no strings attached?

Well, I thought, I don't really care about questions or strings; I'll take my magic any way I can get it. But the 'free' part sounded good, especially since I didn't have any money.

Just fill out our online information form, and you will soon be eligible for a 100% guaranteed free delivery of – you guessed it – MAGIC!!!

Wow. I had no idea it was so easy to get magic! I couldn't believe that I'd stumbled across this site on the first try. Maybe my rotten luck was about to change.

I began to look over the form.

- What is your full address?
- What time of day is your house most likely to be empty?
- Please attach a floor plan of your house.

- Where do you hide your spare key?
- Would you describe your neighbours as
    a) nosy
    b) inclined to mind their own business
    c) willing to help out a stranger who is only trying to get interior decoration ideas in the middle of the night without anyone else knowing?

Once you have emailed us your completed form, just sit back and wait for your magic delivery. Contents will include: an authentic quill from an extinct dodo; a miniature enchanted Stone of Destiny in your choice of three vibrant colours (puce, burnt sienna or goldenrod); and a magic wand hand carved from a yucca brevifolia tree found only in the northern plains of Mexico.

When I came to the last part of the form with the contents of the delivery, the balloon of hope that had been getting bigger and bigger inside of me popped with an almighty bang. *A yucca brevifolia tree?* That just didn't make sense. Everyone knows that wands are made of glass-encrusted, oxidised praseodymium.

No one who had anything to do with real magic would make a mistake like that. Whoever ran this website didn't know what they were talking about. In other words, a fraudster.

This whole thing was clearly a scam.

I went back to the search results page and tried a bunch

of other websites, but there was something a bit dodgy about each of them. One promised to send you a book of magic spells, but the sample spells they quoted were completely bogus (I knew more about spells than these clowns when I was still drinking bat milk from a skull-shaped sippy cup). Another site said it would send you magic potions in the post, but everyone knows that potions have to be made up fresh to be effective.

After trying for ages, I realised that the internet was well and truly a dead end. How could I ever have thought that getting my magic back was going to be easy?

Later that evening, I was still mulling over the whole internet thing, when my mum burst into my room.

"Ruby! Have you taken my little mirror again? It's not in my handbag."

How dare she accuse me of losing her hand mirror! Just because I might mislay things occasionally doesn't mean I should be the only suspect when something goes missing. Anyway, she insisted I find it, so I had to spend 45 minutes tearing my room apart searching for it.

I was still looking when I came across the small wooden chest I kept my most treasured possessions in – it had been the first thing I'd packed when I found out we were leaving the island. I opened it up just in case the mirror had slipped in (which I knew it hadn't, but when you're desperate you'll try anything), and there, along with my souvenir purple cockroach ball from the regional championships, was my old mobile phone. It was small, but it weighed a tonne. Witches' phones are made of lead and encased in bronze to stop any magic interfering with the 4G signal.

Seeing that phone instantly made me think about my friends, and I felt a sharp pang of homesickness. My parents told me when we moved that phones from home don't work here, but surely it couldn't hurt to try it, could it? (Like I said: when you're desperate you'll try anything.)

I selected Abigail's number, and nearly fell over when I heard it ring. Was I *actually* going to talk to one of my friends? I couldn't wait to hear her voice, and tell her how much I missed her, and describe how horrible it was here. Finally, I'd get to talk to someone who understood me...

But no.

An automated message crackled down the line. "You have reached Hexadonian Telecom. If you wish to review your phone bill, please press one. If you would like information about a product recall, please press two. For all other enquiries, please leave a message."

I was disappointed, but I was also confused. Why was the phone company intercepting my best friends' calls?

Then I remembered that all communications from abroad went through the central switchboard on Hexadonia. Maybe if I left a message, they could get it to Abigail or Margaret.

I waited for the beep, and then spoke. "Hi, uh, this is Ruby McCracken. You don't know me, but my mum and dad used to work for the Aerozoom Broom Corporation – Arabella and Stan McCracken? Anyway, I wonder if you could have Abigail Snapdragon or Margaret Darnaway call me. I'm on 55531692048711740829536183574 1. That's in the Ordinary World. Uh… Thank you."

I hung up, and was going to put the phone back in the little chest, but then changed my mind and put it in my pocket. It was heavy without its usual Weightlessness Spell, but I wouldn't want to miss Abigail or Margaret if they phoned back. And besides, it was comforting to have something with me that was a reminder of home.

As I was walking out of my room, something shiny caught my eye. I looked over to the windowsill, and there was my mum's hand mirror, right where I'd left it.

Oops.

CHAPTER 7

I found so many things about the Ords bewildering,
I didn't even know where to begin. Sometimes I felt like
I should be taking notes on their strange ways in case I
ever wanted to publish a guidebook. Actually, that wasn't
a bad idea. I could sell it back home and make a fortune.
No one I knew had ever been to the Ordinary World,
so I'd be an instant expert; I'd be invited on the radio
and on TV to talk about the customs of the natives, and
to give travel advice. I took out my little notebook and
jotted down a few top travel tips:

1. When going to a restaurant in
   the Ordinary World, ask what's
   on the menu, not who.

2. They <u>eat</u> jelly here, instead
   of using it as furniture polish.

3. Flowers are thought to be a good
   thing. Ords actually like them
   (and they heartlessly kill weeds,
   if you can believe it).

4. Instead of tweaking noses to show affection, they press their lips up against someone's face and make a sucking noise. Gross.

5. Speaking of lips, they have something called lipstick, which is like our lobestick, but instead of putting it on their earlobes, they put it on — you guessed it — their lips. I mean... I can't even...

I could also write a mini phrasebook with some of the most commonly-used expressions, such as, "Go back to where you came from, loser!" and "Why are you such a weirdo?" I know these are popular phrases, because people say them to me all the time.

The kids at school, led by the Purple Mafia, seem to be avoiding me. Without anyone to talk to or play with, school is just a glum blur of all the baffling Ord subjects: reading, writing, maths, social studies, French – the terrible list goes on and on. As I'm introduced to each new subject, I find it as puzzling as the one before.

Today, though, things seemed a bit more promising when my class went next door to the high school to have a lesson in chemistry. I guess they're trying to give us a sneak preview for when we move up next year. I can't believe that I'm in the final year of primary school here; back at home, I still had 86 more years to go. I'll never get used to this bizarre system.

When I heard we were going to be doing a real experiment, it got me thinking. Science and magic are kind of similar; they're both about mixing lots of different bits and bobs together until, BANG, you get something completely new. Maybe this could be my chance to get my magic back? Surely it was just a question of getting the right ingredients and heating them up to the right temperature to make a potion...

So I came prepared.

We entered the sleek new building and were led up the stairs to the chemistry labs. Once our classes were split into smaller groups, we all got assigned Bunsen burners with these round glass beakers on top – they're just like miniature cauldrons, really. Fortunately, I didn't have to share my burner with anyone, because everyone else had hastily paired up, and I was the odd one out. Which was a good thing, because I had a job to do.

I hadn't been able to find an eye of a newt, so I used a chocolate frog instead, and I replaced the bat liver with some pâté from the supermarket. For the hyena toenails, I used salt and vinegar crisps – the taste, while not exactly the same, is a pretty close match. When the teacher wasn't looking, I carefully poured the mushed-up ingredients into the beaker and added a big splash of beetroot juice (at least that's the same here).

I heated the concoction up, and watched the thick liquid bubble, as gelatinous lumps of pâté floated to the top. I couldn't wait to try it.

A smell not unlike sweaty gym shoes reached my nostrils, which meant my concoction was finally ready. Glancing round to make sure no one was watching, I noticed Georgia Finnegan staring at me intently. Great, I thought, she was probably getting ready to snitch on me. But before she could say anything, her table partner, Calum Ferguson, suddenly knocked over his beaker, causing a huge fuss; the chemistry teacher ran over to help wipe up the mess as the other students looked on and giggled.

Now was my chance. I whispered the Generic Spell, which may not be the most sophisticated charm I could have chosen, but it's suitable for all occasions, and it's not as though I had many options.

Magic, be thou set in motion
With this swirling liquid potion.

Checking to make sure everyone's attention was still focused on the hullabaloo at Georgia and Calum's table, I took the brown, burbling mixture off the burner. Blowing on it to cool it a bit, I took a big swig. If I'm honest, it wasn't great – a bit gritty for my tastes – but I've had worse. (I must say, it would have been a lot better without the chocolate.) Then, I waited for the fun to begin...

Only, nothing happened.

I drank some more.

Still nothing.

I gulped and gulped until the beaker was empty, but there was no tell-tale tingle or magic-filled burp. The potion was completely devoid of magic. Yet another failed experiment, which is what my whole life was beginning to feel like.

I sank onto the stool next to the table. Despite downing my useless concoction, my tummy was rumbling, so out of habit I mouthed the Snack Spell. But of course, nothing appeared. And why would it? There's no magic in this horrible place.

But that's not even the worst thing. No. The worst thing is that there's no magic in *me*.

When the school day was finally over and I was about to leave, I realised that I'd forgotten to collect my homework jotter. Mum was bound to check, so I went back to get it.

As I pulled the notepad from my tray in the classroom, something slid out from beneath and fell on the floor. It was a sparkly purple envelope. I opened it, and inside was a card with a picture of a pumpkin and a witch's hat on it. In neat, flowing handwriting, it said:

*You are cordially invited to
my spooky Halloween Party,
on Saturday 31st October
from 7 pm until 9 pm.
Please RSVP to Georgia Finnegan.*

I couldn't believe my eyes. *Georgia?* Inviting *me?* To a *party?* How was that possible?

That must have been why she was staring at me in the chemistry lesson. She was probably feeling guilty about being so mean to me in the canteen, and had decided to add me to the guest list at the last minute. Still, an invitation was an invitation. My mum would be so pleased – she really worried about me fitting in. And I couldn't help feeling just an eensy weensy bit pleased myself. Maybe when everyone saw that I'd been invited to Georgia's party, they'd start inviting me to do things with them, too. I imagined what it would feel like not to be alone all the time in the playground and at lunch, and maybe even, who knows, have one or two friends round to my house after school.

Not that I cared about anything like that, of course, but it would be nice for my mum's sake.

I was beginning to make my way to the cloakroom, when I heard the sound of laughter. I looked over and saw Georgia striding down the corridor with her two minions.

"Georgia!" I called.

She stopped and looked at me curiously. "Oh, it's you. What do you want?"

"I just wanted to RSVP to your party invitation. Thank you."

The minions tittered, and Georgia rolled her eyes. "Look, the only reason I invited you is because my parents forced me to invite everyone in the class. So, it's not like I actually *wanted* to." The minions did a really bad job of trying to hold in their sniggers.

I was at a loss for words, literally at a loss – at that moment in time, I didn't have a single word in my head. I felt my face slowly flush as they sneered and giggled.

"So like, whatever," Georgia said, and flicked her hair. This seemed to be the cue for the other two to flick their hair, too, then the three of them flounced off, leaving me standing there by myself, clutching the envelope.

I was furious. I crumpled up the invitation and threw it in the bin. You couldn't pay me to go to Georgia's party, not for all the bat's milk in Boppengubber. And that's *a lot*. I grabbed my cloak and practically ran out of the building. The sooner I could get out of this place, the better.

As I reached the school gate, I heard something I hadn't heard in a long time. It was the sound of fingernails scratching on a chalkboard. At first I didn't realise what it was – then I remembered that it was the sound my phone made when I received a hext. Someone had sent me a hext, an actual hext! Which, thinking about it, was a bit odd, because no one here had my number.

Then I remembered the message I had left with the Hexadonian Telecom switchboard. Could this be Abigail or Margaret?

Trembling with excitement, I reached into the pocket of my blazer and with effort, pulled out my phone. The hext icon glowed on the screen. I tapped it to open the message:

IF U WANT 2 GET YR MAGIC BACK, HXT '6503 MAGIC'. Standard message rates and data fees apply; some calling plans may charge more.

I stared at the words, reading the hext over and over until it didn't make sense any more. Actually, it didn't make sense in the first place. If it wasn't one of my friends, who could be hexting me, and why? How did they get my phone to work? Was it someone from the Ord World, or someone from home?

What if it was just some creepy stranger trying to start up a conversation with me? I'm not a complete idiot; I know you're not supposed to answer hexts from strangers. But I was so curious...

There was only one way to find the answers to my questions. If it turned out to be some weirdo, I would just ignore them. And if it turned out to be one of my friends playing a trick on me, well, it would be a bit of an odd prank, but at least I would get to make contact with them.

Or maybe, there might actually be a way to get my magic back, like *for real*. If so, I *had* to find out how.

With trembling fingers, I typed 6503 MAGIC and waited. Within a few seconds, I heard the fingernail-scratching sound again.

I had received a reply.

CHAPTER 8

I sat down on a bench in the park near school and held my breath as I opened the message. It was quite long – two sets of four lines, and it looked like a poem:

A kingly throne that's way up high,
Where Katie's wheels spin round and round,
Is where you'll see them burn the Guy
With Caesar's candles skyward bound.

Come all to the festive evening.
Bring the family, don't say why.
Soon the magic you'll be weaving
Will enable you to fly.

I must have read every word eight or nine times. The rhyme was a bit dodgy, but clearly, this was a riddle that I had to solve, although I had no idea what it was about. Well, I could at least guess what the second part meant, because it seemed pretty straightforward: I had to bring my family somewhere without telling them why.

A festive evening... that must be a party. Yeah, right; how on earth was that going to work? I imagined myself saying to my mum and dad, "OK guys, we're going to a party, but I can't tell you when or where. You just have to work with me on this. Why? Oh, forgot to mention that I can't tell you why. Let's just say it's because I want us to go, and leave it at that."

Sure, that would go down well.

And we hardly ever went to parties, especially not the whole family together, except maybe to dinner at my parents' friends' houses back home. The kids would eat early, sitting at the breakfast bar, and then we'd go into the living room to play on the Hex Box while the grown-ups ate a leisurely meal at the dinner table, drank blood and chatted about politics and current events. Those didn't exactly count as parties, at least not in my book.

And what about the first part of the riddle? I had no clue. Or I should say, I did have clues, and they were right in front of me, but I couldn't for the life of me figure out how to solve them.

Maybe my parents would know. But if I showed them the hext, I would be disobeying the line that said 'don't say why'. Even worse, they would know that I had replied to a hext from an unknown sender, and they would ground me for approximately 46,000 years.

It was pretty clear that I would have to crack this thing all on my own.

I didn't have the luxury of sitting around thinking about the hext, though, because I had to rush home. After putting up with my mum nagging me for weeks about my social life, I had finally agreed to join something called Girl Guides, just to keep her quiet. Before I caved in, my parents had kept trying to get me to join clubs at school, or even the cricket team. As far as I can tell, cricket is a lot like cockroach, only you don't try to hit people with the ball – so I don't really see the point. And they dress all in white instead of snot green, which just seems wrong.

This Girl Guide compromise seemed to be the least terrible option available to me. Anyway, my mum was so happy when I said I'd try it, she actually volunteered to be a troop leader. I was pretty mortified by this development, but there was no way out.

We arrived at the church hall a few minutes early so my mum could set up. We'd brought sixteen oranges, which she laid out around a table, along with pencils and pots of pens. I tried to skulk in the corner, but she forced me to help.

Just as we were finishing, the girls began arriving. All around my (Ord) age, they eyed my mother warily, and when they saw me in my ski hat, they gave me a funny look too. Fortunately, there was no one from my class there.

As the girls took seats around the table, my mother cleared her throat.

"Hello, girls. I'm Arabella, your new troop leader." She attempted a bright smile, but just ended up looking like she was in pain.

"What happened to our old troop leader, Mrs Mackie?" a voice asked.

My mum paused. "Uh, she's had an... accident."

Several of the girls gasped and three or four spoke at once. "An accident? Is she all right?"

"She's fine," my mother said quickly. "She'll just be... indisposed for a while. Nothing to worry about."

There was a murmur of concern.

"Let's just focus on the present," Mum said. "We're here to have fun!" I knew this kind of enthusiasm didn't come naturally to her, and that she was making a real effort.

Some of the girls shifted uncomfortably in their seats.

"Let's go around the room and introduce ourselves," she continued. "I'm really looking forward to getting to know you. Why don't we each say our name along with something we like that starts with the first letter of our name? For example, if you're called Esmerelda, you might say something like, "I'm Esmerelda, and I like ectoplasm.""

She pointed to an alarmed-looking girl with ginger hair and said, "Why don't you start."

"My name is Claire," the girl said hesitantly, "and I like cakes."

"Cakes? Seriously?" my mum said. "That's kind of weird, but each to her own."

The girls stared blankly at her.

"Right. Next?"

"I'm Isla," the girl next to Claire said, "and I like ice cream."

My mother rolled her eyes. "Come on, girls, you can do better than this. Think of things you *really* like."

"But I *do* like ice cream!" Isla insisted.

"Whatever," Mum said, slightly disappointed.

After everyone had introduced themselves, my mum clapped her hands together and said, "OK, girls, now we're going to do some arts and crafts. You all have a nice, juicy orange in front of you, and some pens. What I want you to do is draw a lovely face on your orange."

The girls began drawing on the oranges.

"If you like, you can try to draw the face of someone close to you. We're going to be giving these as presents, so you might want to draw the person you'll be giving it to."

As the girls set to work, my mum walked around the table murmuring encouragement. "That's a lovely face, Eilidh. Who is it? Your gran? How wonderful! Why don't you add a couple of warts?" And: "Who is that, Maya? Your dad? Why yes, of course – I can see you have his lazy eye. Very realistic."

After several minutes, she called for everyone's attention. "You've all done a brilliant job. There's just one more step. You should have a sharpened pencil in front of you. Does everyone have one? Emma, can you hand that pencil to Catriona? Good. Now, take your orange and stick it on top of the pencil. Push it really hard, like this." My mum demonstrated by stabbing the orange enthusiastically.

The girls looked at one another, unsure.

"Go on," my mum urged, smiling broadly. "You'll see. It'll be lovely."

The girls slowly began to plunge their pencils into their oranges.

"That's excellent, girls," my mum said approvingly. She held hers up for all to see. "And voilà – a head impaled on a stick! You can add little details. See, I've drawn some blood, but you can draw brains spilling out if you like. Use your imagination."

Three or four of the girls started crying, and one fainted.

It was at this moment that the parents arrived to pick up their kids. Let's just say we won't be going back to Girl Guides.

As we took the bus home, my mum and I were each absorbed in our own little world. I couldn't stop thinking about that hext. Who could have sent it? Why did they send it? And, most of all, what did the riddle mean?

I thought about getting my magic back almost every single second of every single minute of every single day.

I spent most of my time at school imagining all the terrible things I would do if I could cast spells on the people who were mean to me. An old favourite was the Athlete's Foot Spell:

No activity is complete
Without flaky, itchy, smelly feet.

Unfortunately, without my hexing skills I'd have to come up with some non-magic ways of giving people fungal infections.

Better yet, I'd have to crack the riddle in the hext. I *needed* to get my magic back and go home.

As the bus trundled down the street, I watched the world go by, lost in thought. Through the buildings, I glimpsed the silhouette of Arthur's Seat rising above the city in the fading light. During the day, especially when the weather was good, you could see people who had climbed up the hill – a small mountain, really – moving around the top like tiny ants.

I mused on the name "Arthur's Seat". I guessed Arthur must be King Arthur, the guy with the Knights of the Round Table – Carl had insisted on watching a stupid TV programme about him at the weekend, so now the whole family knew all about him. As the bus turned onto a smaller street, my mum pressed the STOP button and began collecting her bags of leftover oranges and pencils. She had to jab me in the ribs with her elbow to remind me to get up because I was sitting frozen in my seat.

I had just realised something about the riddle... If Arthur was King Arthur and a throne is a kind of seat, what if Arthur's Seat was the *'kingly throne way up high'* from the hext?

CHAPTER 9

All through school the next day, I tried to work out the rest of the riddle, but the teachers seemed to want me to concentrate on boring *schoolwork*. At lunch and break times, I had to focus so hard on avoiding being shoved into wheelie bins or pelted with footballs by my classmates that I couldn't really work on cracking the code then, either.

As soon as the school bell rang, I hurried straight home to work on solving the riddle in the hext. As I turned onto our street, I noticed three middle-aged women gliding down the pavement on what looked like kids' scooters. Something about them seemed vaguely familiar – they were all wearing big woolly hats. I wondered if they were the same women I'd seen on bicycles a while back. Maybe they were kindly old sisters with an interest in sport who lived in the area? As they scooted past, the one at the end turned her head and looked back at me, giving me a strange grin. She had a huge brown wart on the end of her nose, and something about the look she gave me made a shiver run down my spine. I tried to get a closer look at her face, but by then they had scooted round the corner and out of view. I shrugged, wondering once again why the Ord World was so weird.

I tiptoed into the house without saying hello to anyone and flopped down on the sofa to concentrate. Pulling out my notebook, I wrote down what I knew so far:

1. If I want to get my magic back, I have to somehow convince my family to come to some kind of party on Arthur's Seat.

2. But what if a festive evening isn't a party; what if it means something else? But what?

3. So, to sum up: I have to drag my family to an event of some description, which may or may not be a party.

4. Without telling them why.

5. Which is never going to happen.

6. Sigh.

After a while my head started to hurt, so I went to the kitchen for a drink, where I was greeted by my mum.

"Ah, I see you've come to help with dinner. Carl has a friend over, so we're cooking for five."

So that was why he hadn't been annoying me the moment I stepped through the door – he was off in his room playing with his friend. Carl had already had six or seven play dates since we'd arrived; apparently he was Mr Popularity at our new school. I couldn't for the life of me understand what people saw in him, but there's no accounting for Ord taste.

"The soup's in the cauldron," my mum said. "Why don't you do the salad? There are some stinging nettles from the garden there on the counter, and you can chop up a mouse to throw in. I'll make dessert."

The mention of dessert distracted me from the riddle. "What are we having?" I asked, hoping it was something special.

"Lice pudding."

"Mmm." I love lice pudding; it's fun to see the little critters wriggling on the spoon, and you can still feel them moving around in your stomach hours later.

As I set about preparing the salad, Vronsky lumbered into the kitchen and stopped by his litter tray to cough up a fur ball. Since he was quite a big dog (part Labrador retriever, part sheepdog), he needed a jumbo-sized litter tray, and it had to be cleaned two or three times a day. Back home, Vronsky had liked to hang around the kitchen when Mum was cooking in case she was feeling generous with the rats' tails. Obviously he was remembering this too, and before I could stop him, he jumped up onto the table, sending cutlery crashing to the floor.

"Vronsky!" Mum chided. "Get down." He leapt down and nuzzled my knees sheepishly.

Sometimes I wished Vronsky was still a cat, and wondered if he missed his feline days. It must be hard to suddenly be transformed into a different creature and taken to a completely new environment. Come to think of it, that was kind of how I felt, too.

I shooed Vronsky away with a spare rat's tail to gnaw on and tidied up the mess. As I chopped the salad ingredients, I heard people come into the kitchen. It was my dad with Carl and an angelic-looking, blond-haired little boy.

"This is my sister Ruby," Carl said to the boy. He turned to me. "This is Logan Finnegan."

Finnegan? "Are you any relation to Georgia Finnegan?" I asked.

"She's my sister," the boy said.

This was Georgia Finnegan's *brother*?

Suddenly, I had a terrible thought. What if he mentioned the party invitation? If Mum and Dad found out, there would be no getting out of it. I wouldn't put it past my mum to march me into Georgia's party herself. The Purple Mafia would love that.

As if he could read my mind, Logan cheerfully began to make polite conversation.

"Are you in Georgia's class? You'll be coming to her Hallow—"

Panicking, I grabbed a handful of dried wasps from the bowl on the table and stuffed them into Logan's mouth. "Here, have a snack."

"Ruby!" Mum and Dad gave me a puzzled look.

"What? I'm just being nice to our guest. He looked hungry."

"Wow!" said Logan around a mouthful of wasps. "These are yummy! What are they?"

Bats, this boy was polite. "Erm, they're a new kind of... crisp. Handcooked for extra crunch." From the slop they served in the school canteen, I'd learned that witch foods weren't so popular in the Ord World.

"Hmm, lovely!" he chirruped.

Thankfully, Carl pulled Logan out of the kitchen, although he hissed a "Freak!" in my direction as they left. I turned to my dad, who had gone to the cauldron and was giving the soup a stir.

"What's the deal?" I pointed at Logan's retreating back.

My dad looked up. "What do you mean?"

"I mean, that's Georgia's little brother."

"Who's Georgia?"

"You know, Georgia – the girl in my class." *Who hates my guts*, I added silently.

"Oh, *that* Georgia," Dad said, as though I knew fifteen people with the same name. "The one you don't like. The popular girl."

"That'd be the one," I confirmed.

My dad tasted the soup, and then reached for a little jar of toenail clippings that we keep on a shelf. He sprinkled a few into the simmering pan before speaking. "Huh. That's a coincidence. Because little Logan seems to be quite popular, too. I guess it runs in the family."

I was pondering the fact that only one of us in my family got the popularity gene, and it sure wasn't me, when my mum interrupted my pity party for one. "Is the salad ready?"

"Yep," I replied.

"Dressing?" she asked.

"Oh. No, you didn't tell me to make dressing."

My mum shook her head. "Do I have to spell everything out?"

"I'm not a mind reader." There was silence. "Well, not any more."

I quickly made some dressing out of frogspawn juice, curdled milk and a hint of powdered bat wing, which we'd brought from back home, while my dad poured the soup into a tureen. Mum called Carl and Logan back into the kitchen, and they began putting out bowls and salad plates.

"Logan, why don't you sit down. That's Carl's job, and you're a guest," my dad said.

"I don't mind, Mr McCracken," Logan said cheerfully.

I marvelled at how different this boy was from his big sister. Or maybe he was just like her, and was putting on a front for his friend's parents? That was probably it.

73

We all took our seats. The black soup tureen sat at one end of the table near my dad, and the big salad bowl was down at the other end near my mum.

We all waited.

Finally, Logan said to my dad, "Erm, can I have some soup, please?"

"Of course," Dad replied, staring at the soup tureen.

"Dad?" Carl prompted as Dad continued staring intently at the soup tureen. I could tell he had forgotten that our food doesn't serve itself any more.

"You actually have to serve it, Dad," I reminded him.

"Ah, yes; forgive me." He hurriedly ladled soup into Logan's bowl.

The rest of the meal proceeded uneventfully, until Logan asked for salad, and then it was Mum's turn to stare maniacally at the serving dish, willing it to fly across the table. I cleared my throat loudly until she finally got the hint and passed the dish to Logan.

At that moment, Vronsky jumped up onto Logan's lap. You could hardly see the boy beneath the giant, furry creature.

"What a friendly dog," came Logan's muffled voice, although I could tell he was struggling to breathe.

"Vronsky, down!" my dad shouted, shooing him off Logan. Vronsky pattered across the kitchen floor, his thick claws clattering over the tiles. With some effort, he hauled himself onto the window sill, where he perched awkwardly, his hind quarters hanging over the sink.

74

"He likes to look out the window," Mum explained.

"At the birds," Carl added.

"Cool," Logan said.

"Who has room for dessert?" my mother asked, bringing the lice pudding to the table. "Logan?"

Logan nodded eagerly.

This time, Mum remembered to spoon out the pudding, and it was gone in a flash.

"Ooh, this feels tingly in my tummy," Logan said.

"It's..." my mum began.

"...a special recipe," I cut in.

As we sat contentedly digesting our dinner, Dad suggested we play a game of darts.

"That sounds like fun," Logan said.

Mum went to the living room to get them from the bookshelf, then opened the case to reveal a dozen silver darts with thick, gleaming needles.

"Where's the dart board?" Logan asked.

"We take turns," Mum replied.

Logan nodded. "You take turns throwing the darts?"

"No," I corrected him, "we take turns being the dart board."

"Since you're our guest, you can have the first go," Mum said brightly.

Logan blanched. He was already pale to begin with, but now you could see right through him.

"I know," Carl said quickly, seeing Logan's distress, "why don't we play Snakes and Ladders?"

Logan smiled weakly.

"OK, Snakes and Ladders it is." Mum headed for the cupboard under the stairs. "I'll just be two tics."

A minute later, my mum came back in carrying a large box, and placed it on the floor. I helped her lift the lid.

"Are those...?"

"Alive?" Mum said, taking hold of one of the colourful snakes, which wriggled in her hands. "Yep."

I glanced over at Logan, expecting to have to catch him when he fainted. But instead, I saw a beaming little boy.

"Awesome!" he cried.

CHAPTER 10

The next day was another busy one at school. We had a baking lesson and made fruit scones, and even though I tried to convince myself that the raisins were flies, it was no use; the scones were disgusting. I was so repulsed by them that I felt sick, and I actually forgot about the hext.

And then, just when I started thinking about it again, Ms MacLean announced, "Children, I have a surprise for you all..."

The class went silent with anticipation. What could it be, I wondered? Would she be handing out frogs' intestines as a little reward for working so hard? Would she send us home early with no homework? Would we be going on a fun school trip to a snail farm (yummy), or maybe even a medieval Edinburgh dungeon?

Well, I guessed right that we'd be going on a trip, but sadly I was wrong about the fun part. Never in a million years could I have guessed where. No, I take that back – I actually *could* have guessed if you'd asked me to name the last place in the world I wanted to go:

Ms MacLean continued, "Next week I'm taking you all on a class trip to the famous aquarium, Deep Sea World!"

Deep Sea World. That was the big surprise – we were going to an aquarium. All that water... I couldn't bear to even think about it.

It was a good thing I had the riddle to distract me from thinking too much about the horror of our impending trip. As soon as school was out, I was able to devote my full attention to it.

I had read it so many times now that I knew it by heart:

A kingly throne that's way up high,
Where Katie's wheels spin round and round,
Is where you'll see them burn the Guy
With Caesar's candles skyward bound.

Come all to the festive evening.
Bring the family, don't say why.
Soon the magic you'll be weaving
Will enable you to fly.

I'd pretty much cracked the second half of the riddle, but the majority of the first one was giving me a lot of trouble. I was still thinking about it when I got home.

My dad was sitting in the kitchen leafing through the newspaper and idly carving a picture on the table with a pen knife. I'd always thought he was a frustrated artist at heart.

"Hi Dad," I said as I grabbed a dried wasp from a bowl on the table.

"Hi," he said absently, absorbed in the paper.

I took another wasp, and then another. It's impossible to stop at just one, they're so... crackly.

When I walked into the living room, I saw Carl sitting at the computer, which was making a loud whirring noise.

"Hey," I said.

"Uh-huh," he muttered, as absorbed by what he was doing as Dad was.

I sat on the sofa munching my wasps and contemplated the hext again, but I was distracted by the noise the computer was making.

"You know," I said to Carl, "you're not even supposed to be on the computer. I'm going to tell Dad."

"Dad knows," he said matter-of-factly.

"Oh, he does, does he? He knows you're on the computer before you've finished your homework?"

"This *is* my homework, bludderfig," he smirked.

"Yeah, right, you gab-faced little grottlebud." Carl should know better than to mess with me when it comes to name-calling.

"It is. It's a presentation I have to do on 'Fun Facts about Scotland'."

"Yep," my dad said, wandering into the living room, "I'm sure you'll be able to teach us a thing or two!"

"OK, wise guy," I said, "give us a fun fact about Scotland. Something we don't already know."

Carl squinted and thought for a moment. Finally he said, "The national flower of Scotland is the thistle."

"Thistle leaves have spikes, you know," Dad said.

"I know. Isn't that cool?" said Carl.

"We all know what a thistle is. Did you learn anything else about Scotland, pinhead?" I asked.

He scowled at me. "Edinburgh is the capital."

"Very good, Carl," Dad said.

I rolled my eyes. Boy, it sure didn't take much to impress your parents when you were eight (or 192 in witch years).

"Anything else?"

"Hmm. Let's see. New Year's Eve is called Hogmanay, and they have lots of fireworks. Like Skyrockets, Roman candles, Catherine wheels..."

"Huh, fireworks?" my dad said. "You know fireworks are a source of magic for witches."

"Even in the Ord World?" Carl asked. He was getting excited.

"Even in the Ord World," Dad replied. "They make spells work here, which they wouldn't otherwise, because as you know, magic doesn't normally work in the Ord World. Something about all the condensed energy in fireworks activates magic. You need a lot of them, though."

Now my ears pricked up. "Really? Does that mean we can get magic on New Year's Eve?"

My dad chuckled, but he didn't look happy. "Sadly, no.

Not us. You have to have some magic in the first place, which means keeping up with the magic bills. Which we, er, haven't..."

I wondered how whoever sent the hext was planning to help me get my magic back when I didn't pay any magic bills myself. Maybe they'd pay them for me?

"We don't have to wait 'til Hogmanay, though," Carl chimed in.

I looked at him. "What do you mean?"

"They have fireworks on Bonfire Night, too."

"What's 'Bonfire Night'?"

"It's where they burn a dummy of a man called Guy Fawkes, because he tried to blow up the Houses of Parliament hundreds of years ago or something. Sounds pretty cool!"

I sat up straight as a rod. "What did you say his name was?"

"Guy Fawkes."

"Yes!" I yelled, trying hard not to whoop with glee. Guy Fawkes! That must be what 'burn the Guy' meant in the hext. The evening party was Bonfire Night!

Carl stared at me as though I was crazy. "What's your problem?"

"I'm just happy, that's all." Understatement of the year.

My dad frowned. "You know, kids, why don't you get your homework done before your mum gets home."

"Mine's all done," Carl said. Of course it was.

They both headed off to the garden to kick Jeremy

around so I could focus on my 'homework,' but there was no way I could concentrate on something as boring as that when I had the riddle to think about. As I was mulling it over, Vronsky clattered into the room.

"Hey Vronsk." I scratched his head. He growled, but I knew that was just his canine way of purring.

"You want to help me solve this riddle?" I asked, and he put his paw on my knee in reply.

"OK, I'm trying to figure out the first part of the poem. I know that the *kingly throne that's way up high* is Arthur's Seat."

Vronsky wagged his tail.

"But what about *Katie's wheels* and *Caesar's candles*?"

Vronsky cocked his head to one side and looked at me curiously.

"What?"

He continued looking at me, as though he were waiting for me to figure something out. I thought about the fireworks show, and then slapped my forehead.

"Of course! Katie is short for Catherine, and Carl said Catherine wheels are a kind of firework!"

Vronsky leapt onto the sofa and nuzzled his face into my shoulder in celebration.

"But what about Caesar's candles?"

Vronsky stopped leaping, and sat next to me, motionless. I racked my brains. *Caesar, Caesar.* Wasn't that the guy with leaves on his head that Ms MacLean had gone on about for ages in class the other week? If only I'd actually been listening. Some of it must have gone in... What did I know about Caesar? He was a Roman – that was about it. No, wait – that *was* it! I looked at Vronsky.

"Caesar was a Roman, Vronsk!" I screeched. "Don't you remember? Carl was just saying that Roman candles are a kind of firework. This is definitely about a fireworks display!"

That was it – I'd cracked the riddle! "Yessity yes!" I tried to pick up Vronsky and spin him around, but he was so heavy I had to put him back down with a thud. "I'm going to get my magic back!" I cried. "We're going to go home!" Vronsky growled happily, licked my face for good measure, and then lumbered off.

But my excitement was short-lived. I sank onto the sofa. Once I began to reflect on the situation, I realised that although I might have solved the clues, I somehow still had to get my family to Arthur's Seat on Bonfire Night during the fireworks. Without telling them why. Just as I was wondering how on earth I could possibly do this, I heard the front door open.

It was my mum. She was wearing a funny orange-and-white cap made of paper, by the look of it. Without a word, she came over to the sofa and tweaked my nose. Then, as Carl and Dad entered the living room, she tweaked Carl's nose too.

Dad looked at her nervously. "How'd it go?"

Mum smiled the biggest smile I think I've ever seen.

"You got the job?" my father cried.

"Yes!"

Dad ran over to Mum and tweaked her nose happily. "That's brilliant! I knew you would."

She delicately touched her orange-and-white hat. "And look – the best part of all. I get to wear this!"

"Wow," my brother breathed in awe, "that's beautiful."

My mother beamed. "I know, right?"

I realised that I was going to have to set aside the incredible excitement of having cracked the riddle and participate in this little moment of family happiness. "So where is this new job?" I asked, to be polite. I know it's an awful thing to say, but at that moment, I didn't really care about anything but the hext.

"Burger Barn," my mum said proudly. "Here, I'll show you." She cleared her throat and tilted her head as though she was going to say something profound. "May I take your order?"

"I can see why you got the job," Dad said. "You're a natural."

"OK, OK, enough about me. I want to hear about how *you* are all doing." She turned to me. "How was your day, Slimeball?"

"It was fine, just fine. Actually, there's something I want to—"

"Did you get any homework?"

"Homework? Yeah, I think I did. But I just wanted to—"

"Did you write the assignment down?"

"Write it down? Of course I did." Why was she going on

about my homework when there were so many more important things to talk about?

"Great. Can I see it?"

"Sure," I rifled through my backpack for my homework jotter so that I could show her and move on to the topic of Bonfire Night. "It's just in my—"

But then I realised that the jotter wasn't in my backpack. I had accidentally left it in my tray at school.

Observing me, my mum asked with mock innocence, "It's in your what?"

"It's in my homework jotter," I mumbled.

"Which, let me guess, you've lost?"

"I haven't lost it!" I said automatically. "It's at school."

"Ruby McCracken, I cannot believe you've lost something *again*," she sighed, but her eyes were twinkling. "If I weren't so thrilled about this new job, I'd be really angry. But I'm not going to let anything ruin this night."

"I didn't lose it!" I tried again. "It's merely been temporarily mislaid."

"Oh Ruby." My mother took off her hat and placed it carefully on the coffee table. "What are we going to do with you?"

"You don't have to do anything with me."

"No, we do," my dad chimed in, "or you'd lose yourself. You'd wake up one morning and say, 'Now what did I do with myself?'"

"Ha ha," I said, even though I did not find this in the least bit funny.

Carl then decided to join in the Ruby Attackfest. "I bet you couldn't go for a week without losing something."

"A whole week? Don't be ridiculous," my mother said.

"A week? That's *so* easy," I shrugged.

"Really?" Dad chimed in. "Care to put your money where your mouth is?"

"Now, that's an idea," said Mum. "If you can go for a whole week without losing anything, I'll give you... hmm, let me see. I know – how about a bicycle?"

"Hey, that's not fair!" Carl said.

"Don't worry," Dad told him. "It'll never happen."

I couldn't believe how little faith they had in me.

"Oh, it'll happen," I smirked.

"Yeah, well," Carl sniffed, "even if they do give you a bike, they'll probably just take it away again, like they did with that cool broom I got for my last birthday."

My mum gave my dad a significant look before saying gently to Carl, "Slimeball, you *know* we couldn't let you keep the Sparkler. It wasn't quite right for you, remember? The one we replaced it with was much better."

"It seemed fine to me." Carl was still clearly miffed about having his birthday present taken off him. Although it *had* made some funny whirring noises.

While Carl was yammering on about speed functions and aerodynamics, I had an idea. "I don't want a bike," I said.

"I'll have it!" piped in Carl.

"What do you want?" Mum looked intrigued.

I couldn't believe it; the perfect opportunity had just

fallen right into my lap. "I want us to go to Arthur's Seat on Bonfire Night to watch the fireworks."

My mum and dad looked at each other. I could tell they were checking to see what the other thought. They can't seem to go to the toilet without consulting with the other one first these days.

Leaning their heads together in a parental pow-wow, they started muttering, but I could hear most of what they were saying.

"Fireworks?" Mum was mumbling. "You're sure it's OK?"

My dad nodded. "There'll be lots of people. There aren't any blah blah blah blah."

I didn't get all of that sentence.

"But aren't they blah blah blah?"

Seriously, didn't anyone teach them to enunicate?

"No. They can't blah blah here."

Oh, I give up.

"Well, if you're sure." My mother turned to me, looking a little unconvinced. "It's a deal," she said. "We'll have an inspection a week from today."

As we tweaked on it, Vronsky clattered back into the room and leap towards me, growl-purring like a tractor, and began to lick my face. I only just managed to stay on my feet. Now I, too, was deliriously happy. I couldn't believe I was going to get my magic back, and all I had to do was not lose anything for a week!

I mean, how hard could that be?

CHAPTER 11

Turns out my mum liked her orange-and-white paper hat so much that she wore it everywhere. It was incredibly embarrassing when she picked me up at school one day for a dentist appointment wearing her Burger Barn hat. Not the whole uniform – which would have been OK because it would have looked like she was coming straight from work – just her normal clothes and the hat. Mrs Stobo in the school office took one look at her and said, "Oh, I see where Ruby gets her fondness for headgear."

Mum touched her hat and smiled. "Thank you."

I wanted to disappear. But sadly, I couldn't. Yet another thing I couldn't do without magic.

My dad also managed to find a new job, sweeping the floor in a hairdressers. I visited him there on Saturday, and saw the way he looked longingly at the broom and then out the window at the sky. Poor guy. At least he started bringing free samples home from work, which was just as well because I like to use a lot of gel in my hair to keep it looking slick. I go for the greasy look; Mum says you could fry chips in my hair. I try to keep showering to a bare minimum, since I *hate* water, so it's easier to keep this way. I mean, drinking water's OK (I'm not planning to die of dehydration, obviously), but I draw the line at unnecessary hygiene.

Now that my mum and dad both had jobs, it was a relief not to have to worry so much about money, though we weren't rich by any means. But I could tell my parents were still concerned about one thing – my lack of friends. My mum was especially worried, so one evening I decided to tell her about the invitation to Georgia's party. I'd already decided I wasn't going, but I thought it would reassure her to know that I was at least getting invited to things (OK, "thing," singular). It would make her think my social life was starting to pick up and get her off my case. Then I'd inform her casually that I'd decided not to go, and that way, I could have my mosquito-cake and eat it.

It didn't work out that way, though. Once I'd mentioned the invitation, my mum got really excited. I mean, I knew she would get excited, but not *this* excited.

"Oh Slimeball, that's wonderful!" She came over to where I was sitting on the couch and gave me a huge tweak on the nose.

"It's no big deal," I said. "Everybody in my class is invited."

"Still, it's a chance for you to socialise with people outside of school, which is great. When people are in school, they feel a bit hemmed in by all the rules and the teachers and things. When they're away from school, they feel freer to be themselves."

"Yeah, maybe, but anyway, I've decided not to go."

My mum sat up straight. "*What?*"

I could tell by her tone that this was not going to end well.

"I've decided not to go. Georgia only invited me because her mum made her."

"Her mother was right," Mum said firmly.

"Well, she may have been right, but that doesn't mean I'm going." I crossed my arms to show her I meant business.

"Oh, you're going."

"But Georgia's really mean! You should see the way she—"

"She was kind enough to extend an invitation to you, and it will be a great chance to get to know your classmates. You're going. I will not discuss it any more."

"I will not discuss it any more" really meant, "My decision is final, and nothing you say will make me change my mind."

With that, my mum walked out of the room.

So I was going to be spending Halloween at Georgia Finnegan's house, where I'd probably end up sitting in a corner bored out of my mind, watching Georgia and her purple pets make fun of me. And on this, the most important night of the year for us witches.

Halloween back home was the best, and I mean *the best*. We always got a Halloween calendar, and Carl and I would take turns eating the candied toad livers. We'd hang a festive wreath of poison ivy on the front door, and Halloween songs would float through the air.

In the evening, we would fly around in groups, showing off the stunts we'd been practising all year. My mum and dad's speciality was a quadruple somersault, and I was working on an awesome double half-flip when we moved. Even Carl was starting to develop a slalom manoeuvre, which frankly isn't a big deal, but then he's only young (and it's probably quite difficult for someone with such a tiny head). The whole evening always culminated in some synchronised flying, where we'd link arms and make shapes in the air with all our brooms together. The first year we'd done this, we'd started out with a basic pentacle formation, but by last year we were making a dodecahedron while waving flares.

After the fly-overs, we'd have people round to our house for food and games. My father would always roast an alligator on the spit in our back garden, and my mum would make her famous tree-bark soup and some deadly nightshade salad, and there would be mosquito cake and ice blood for dessert. The one not-so-great thing was that Carl and I were always forced to perform a duet – Carl played the harpsichord, and I banged on Carl's head in time to the music – but once that ordeal was over, we would put on some records and dance round the cauldron to *real* music. Then it would be time for games, my favourite part of the evening. We would play bobbing for frogs, pass the potion, musical electric chairs, and pin-the-skull on the skeleton.

So, in other words, Halloween was a big deal – and going

to Georgia's party was apparently a *done* deal. Since it was clear there was no way out, I would just have to go with it. And after thinking about it for a while, I decided that just because Georgia didn't want me to be there, that didn't mean I couldn't enjoy myself. I could always pretend I was an anthropologist studying the customs of an alien culture.

I had told my mum that, in the Ord Halloween tradition, it was customary to wear a fancy-dress costume, which meant we had to go shopping. Fortunately, there are lots of shops in Edinburgh.

Before we left the house, Mum stepped into the back garden to ask my Dad and Carl if they wanted to come with us. They were kicking Jeremy around.

Dad looked at Carl. "What do you think, son? Stay here playing skullball, or go shopping with your mother and sister?"

"That's a no-brainer." Then Carl said to Jeremy, "Oh, sorry. No offence."

"No worries," Jeremy tutted. "But now that we're on the subject, I wouldn't say no to a spot of shopping myself."

My dad looked down at Jeremy. "No one asked you."

"No one ever asks me," Jeremy sighed.

"Have a good time," Dad called to us, and kicked Jeremy through a goal that he and my brother had made out of rocks.

"But I haven't been shopping in centuries..." I could hear Jeremy whimper as he sailed past the goal.

We would have left earlier, but I spent ten minutes searching for my bag, all the while pretending that I needed the toilet. I couldn't let my mum know that I'd *already* lost something, or the Bonfire Night deal would be off.

"Are you OK?" Mum was clearly concerned when I disappeared for what seemed to be my third trip to the bathroom.

"Fine," I called from the back of the house, as I frantically searched my bedroom yet again. I finally found the bag under my bed, and emerged triumphant into the living room, muttering something about having eaten too many fruit flies the night before.

"I told you to stop after the first handful."

"Well, now I know."

"You would have known sooner if you'd just listened to me," Mum scolded as we walked out the door. I was too traumatised from my near miss with the lost bag to answer back.

We took the bus down to Princes Street and went to a big department store. We had to walk through the tableware section to get to the escalator. As we passed a fancy display of place settings, my mother paused to examine something, before turning to me.

"I've got it. I know what you can go as." She looked very pleased with herself.

"What?"

She held up a piece of cutlery and said triumphantly, "A fork!"

"A fork? How would that work?" Seriously, sometimes I wondered about my mum.

"Let's see. You'd need to get some metal for the tines, and wrap your legs together to look like the part you hold, and then—"

"Stop right there. I am not going to Georgia Finnegan's Halloween party dressed as a fork!"

"OK, suit yourself." She put the utensil down, disappointed.

We walked on in silence, but just as we were about to get on the escalator, she stopped again, this time at a stationery display.

"I know," she said. "A pencil case."

"What? You want me to go as a pencil case?" I said incredulously. "Mum! Don't you understand? You need to go as some *one*, not some *thing*."

"Oh," she said testily. "Why didn't you tell me that? OK, let's go to the third floor."

As we spoke, we walked past the sports department, and I looked wistfully at the cricket bats and balls – it wasn't quite the same as cockroach, but there were enough similarities to make me feel nostalgic. When we passed the exercise equipment, I noticed something odd: there were those three women I'd seen before, now dressed in hoodies, but still wearing massive hats. One was on an exercise bike, one on a treadmill and the third on a rowing machine. They all looked a bit sweaty and out of breath. The taller one with the wart was rowing

94

unenthusiastically, but stopped dead when she saw me. She jumped up to whisper something to the small, bespectacled woman on the treadmill, who stopped running to listen to her, but the treadmill kept going and she tumbled to the floor. The third woman, who had black curls peeking out from under her hat, clambered down from the exercise bike to help her friend up. The tall, warty one just glared at me. Why? Why did these people seem so interested in me?

I turned to point all this out to my mum, but she had already stepped on to the escalator going up to the next floor. I had to scurry to catch up with her, so I put my concerns about the strange women to the back of my mind.

As we walked past various clothing displays, Mum asked me what kinds of things people usually dress up as.

"Things they think are frightening," I said, "like... I don't know, ghosts."

"Aww, how sweet!" she exclaimed.

"Or vampires."

"You didn't tell me Halloween was such a *charming* holiday here."

"Well, I've just been overhearing people talk about what they're going as. And Frankenstein, that's another popular one."

"Charlie Frankenstein? Victor Frankenstein's boy?"

"Yep."

"But he's such a nice kid."

"And zombies – they're pretty popular, too."

"I don't care much for zombies," my mother sniffed. "They're a bit twee, if you ask me."

I suddenly remembered something. "Oh, and get this. You know what the most popular costume of all is?"

"If it's not forks or pencil cases, then I'm out of ideas."

"*Witches.*"

My mum's eyes widened, and I swear I saw what must have been the same idea enter her head at the same time it popped into mine.

"I know," she said, "why don't you wear your old school uniform?"

I had begged my mum to let me bring my uniform with us. She had argued at first, but when she saw how much it meant to me, she caved in. I knew it would come in handy!

All I said was, "My thoughts exactly." I guessed it was probably not a good idea to say *I told you so*.

As we waited for the bus home, I felt really happy. If someone had told me that the prospect of wearing my old school uniform would one day fill me with joy, I would have said they were crazy. But now, just imagining wearing it again made me feel a little bit more like *myself*. It's funny what being uprooted and dragged to a new place against your will can do to you.

"You're in a good mood," Mum observed. "Excited about your school trip tomorrow?"

And that was all it took to bring me crashing back

to reality. My school trip. Why did she have to go and bring that up?

How could I possibly be anything other than horrified at the thought of my school trip? A place surrounded by water, in the company of people who made every day miserable? It was going to be the worst day of my life. Well, the second-worst day – the absolute worst day, of course, was the day we left our old lives behind to move to this unspeakably horrible place.

CHAPTER 12

I used to love school trips. We went to so many cool places with my old school. Like the Archipelagic Library, a grand building with beautiful murals depicting important events from the history of the Hexadonian Archipelago. Or the pumpkin museum – that was really fun, and we all got to carve a screaming face into a pumpkin and take it home at the end.

Once we even went to my mum and dad's work, which was weird and embarrassing, but I was just a teensy bit proud when they each talked about what they did. We even got to tour the broom factory. It actually wasn't as boring as it sounds; it was pretty cool to see the brooms flying off the assembly line, and the factory workers chasing after them to package them up.

But of all the places we could have gone, Deep Sea World was the worst.

The morning of the trip, I pleaded, "Couldn't I just not go? I could pretend to be sick. Or I could say I'm allergic to sea life."

"In this family, we do not lie," my mum said.

"How can you say that?" I looked from her to my dad. "Have you forgotten that you posed as foreign dignitaries, using fake passports, when we moved here?"

"That's different," Mum said sternly.

"How is it different?" I folded my arms.

"It just is," my dad snapped, and I could tell from his voice that this was the end of the conversation. Again.

"I can't wait to go to Deep Sea World," Carl chimed in from the breakfast bar, where he was finishing his thorn flakes (our very last packet from home. Pig.).

"Look," Dad told me, "you probably won't actually come into contact with water. Just because it's called Deep Sea World doesn't mean you have to go swimming with dolphins or anything."

He had a point. I just needed to remember that I was going there to *observe* sea life, not participate in it.

On the coach ride over to Deep Sea World though, it did feel like I was locked in a pen with a bunch of wild animals. Even though Ms MacLean was with us, she was busy playing a game on her phone the whole time and didn't seem to notice all the mayhem going on around her.

I sat on my own and focused on not being sick (I still wasn't used to travelling around in Ord vehicles). As we drove over the Firth of Forth on our way to North Queensferry, I admired the view of the Forth Rail Bridge and, beyond that, a tiny island with a ruined abbey on it. It reminded me a little of home; I used to fly over the Briladeem of Shalamanthia on my way to school every day, and there were a couple of little islands there, much smaller than the one we lived on, which had ruined castles on them. The dull ache of missing home made my nausea even worse.

Finally, the coach pulled into a car park, and we all filed off the bus.

"OK, guys," Ms MacLean announced. "You know the drill. We queue up at the entrance and wait until our guide arrives. No running, lagging behind, shouting, whispering, eating or drinking while on the tour."

"So basically, no opposites," someone said.

"And most of all, no smart alecs," Ms MacLean replied with a stern stare.

We walked in silence to the entrance of the building, passing a pool with little remote-controlled electric boats in it. I thought of the nineteen-day boat journey we had taken to get to Scotland. The memory of spending all that time surrounded by water made me shudder.

At the entrance, we were greeted by a guy in glasses who couldn't have been long out of high school, and who introduced himself as Ewan. He led us round, showing us various tanks filled with assorted weird-looking sea creatures. In one tank, dozens of multi-coloured clown fish swam back and forth while a lone blue fish circled endlessly. I could identify with that blue fish, far from its natural habitat, surrounded by clowns.

My tummy rumbled, and I remembered that I hadn't eaten much for breakfast because I was so nervous about the trip. I mouthed the Snack Spell silently, out of habit, even though I knew nothing would come of it. It always made me feel a little better in times of crisis.

The group had now arrived at a shallow open tank. The guide indicated to people to gather round, and he began talking about the various creatures inside it.

"And who knows what this little guy is called?" He lifted a five-armed creature out of the water. "I'll give you a hint. He's often followed by the paparazzi!" The guide laughed at his own joke, and looked at the class expectantly.

"A pentacle fish," I said automatically. I couldn't help myself; we have them back home.

"No... but that's close," the guide said. "It's a starfish. Here, would you like to hold it?" He began to hand the slippy, soaking wet creature to me, but I shrank back in horror.

"Get that thing away from me!" I shouted and reeled back.

The guide shrugged and handed the starfish to one of my classmates.

Ms MacLean leaned over and whispered to me, "I know how you feel. I'm squeamish around all these beasties, too."

"It's not the fish," I said. "It's the water. I *hate* the stuff. Absolutely hate it."

Ms MacLean looked a bit surprised, but then nodded sympathetically. She must be used to dealing with all kinds of kids' phobias. Carl said there was a boy in his class who was even scared of spiders. Weirdo.

At that moment, I heard a titter. I turned around and saw the Purple Mafia attempting to stifle a giggle, about as successfully as when I had tried to RSVP to Georgia's party invitation. Well, not all of the Purple Mafia were laughing. Georgia herself was silent. She was staring at me again with a strange expression, as though I were a code she was trying to crack. I thought about asking if she wanted a picture of me so she could stare at it all she wanted, but then thought better of it. I didn't want to end up going for an 'accidental' swim.

After what seemed like hours, we moved on to the next part of the tour, which was a huge transparent tunnel through the water where you could stand and watch fish swimming over your head. Well, other people could do that, but I certainly wasn't going anywhere near the Tunnel of Terror. I hung back and retraced my steps, hoping to find an alternative route that didn't involve so much water.

After what seemed like an eternity, everyone emerged from the tunnel and it was finally time for lunch. Thankful for an opportunity to get away from all the wet stuff, I scurried over to the cafeteria and joined the queue. There wasn't much of a choice, but they had fish and chips (which struck me as a little bit cannibalistic in a place devoted to fish-worshipping, but then these are Ords we're talking about, and logic isn't their strong point). I've noticed that people here like their chips, and seem to eat them with everything. I've found them to be almost palatable, as long as I close my eyes and pretend they're fried slugs; crunchy on the outside and soft on the inside.

I ate alone, surprise surprise, and pretended to be busy reading loads of messages on my phone, when in fact I was re-reading the one hext message that I'd received since coming to the Ord World, over and over again. There were only a few days to go before my week of not losing things was up, and although I'd had several *very* close calls, I hadn't actually lost anything. I couldn't believe I was so close to possibly getting what I wanted most in the world. I thought of all the things magic would allow me to do that I hadn't been able to since we arrived here. I wondered how it would work – if I'd get to use magic in the Ord World, or if I'd be whisked back home. I thought about what would happen to my family. Surely I wouldn't be expected to go back all by myself? Surely they'd all come with me? I wondered if I'd know where to go on Bonfire Night, or even what I should be looking for when the time came. Would there be some kind of signal, someone to meet? Then I started wondering – not for the first time – who had sent the hext message. To break through the barrier between home and the Ord World, it must have been some big fish in the sorcery world. None of my friends from back home would have been able to do that. But why would someone who didn't know me try to help me?

When lunch was over, Ms MacLean allowed us a brief visit to the gift shop (I didn't buy anything – why would I want a souvenir to remind me of all this water?), and then she bustled us onto the coach. After a quick head count, the bus set off. I sat alone again. Nothing new there. Ms MacLean was sitting on the back seat, supposedly so she could keep an eye on all of us, but I knew she was engrossed in her game of Monster Truck Mash-Up.

I closed my eyes and tried to focus on not getting sick. I silently mouthed the words of the Happy Tummy incantation over and over. The funny thing was, it seemed almost as effective without magic as it was with.

All of a sudden, I felt something on my head. Or, to be more precise, I felt something come *off* my head: my fleece hat. I opened my eyes and turned around. Rachel, the taller of Georgia Finnegan's purple minions, was twirling my hat in the air as if it were pizza dough. Lots of people were laughing.

I looked to the back of the bus, but Ms M was still staring at her phone. I made a lunge for the hat, but then Rachel threw it to Calum across the aisle. I leaned over to grab it, but then Calum threw it to Lewis. I couldn't take it any longer. I put my hands over my ears and just sat like that for the rest of the journey. If they wanted to see me cry, they'd be waiting a long time.

When the coach pulled up to the school, I grabbed my backpack and pushed to the front so I could be the first one off. I wasn't staying with these horrible Ords a minute longer than I had to.

But as soon as I reached the classroom, I realised that I had forgotten to see if my hat was still on the bus. I ran back to the car park, now pushing past people going the other way.

When I got there, the bus was gone.

And along with it, my hat.

CHAPTER 13

I found Ms MacLean walking towards the classroom, and stopped her to tell her that I'd left my hat on the bus. At first she told me to go back to class, but I persisted.

"Can we call the bus company? Maybe it's still on the bus."

"Don't worry." She patted my arm reassuringly. "It will turn up."

"How do you know?" I didn't share her positive outlook.

"These things always do. I'm sure someone took it by mistake."

I remembered the hat being thrown from seat to seat. Yeah right, someone took it by 'mistake'.

"Just check in Lost Property tomorrow," she continued.

"But what if—"

"Ruby, class is starting. Just check in Lost Property tomorrow." Ms MacLean's sympathy was wearing thin.

We only had about thirty minutes left before school officially ended, which was a good thing, because I was freaking out. Ms MacLean put on a film about dental hygiene, which was also a good thing, because I felt like

I was going to cry, and I would *not* have wanted people to see that. I tried to focus on the film. I marvelled at the fact that people here try to *prevent* their teeth from rotting and falling out, whereas back where I'm from, the more gaps the better.

But even fascinating pictures of people cleaning their teeth couldn't distract me from my troubles for long. How would I ever get my magic back now that I'd lost my hat and the bet with my mum? And besides, I felt naked without my hat. I got out my notebook and thought about my options:

1. Tell Mum what happened, and hope for forgiveness. It wasn't my fault someone took my hat.

2. Don't tell Mum and hope the hat will turn up.

3. Buy a new hat exactly the same so she won't realise I've lost it.

Then I thought about the pros and cons of each option.

Option 1:

Pro: Telling Mum will give me the chance to tell her my side of the story.

Pro: I'll get points for honesty.

Con: It'll reveal to her how deeply unpopular I really am, which might upset her.

Option 2:

Pro: Not telling Mum is the easiest option. I've still got three days left before the big inspection, and maybe it will turn up between now and then.

Con: What if it doesn't turn up?

Option 3:

Pro: Buying a new hat would be an easy option if I had money.

Con: I don't.

I decided that option number two, not telling my mum for now, was my best bet; at least it would buy me some time. The bus company might hand in the hat to Lost Property. All I had to do now was fob my mum off until then. No problem.

I found this thought immensely cheering, and stopped feeling like I wanted to cry. Just when I was learning about the importance of brushing your tongue (Your tongue! Who knew?), the bell rang, and people streamed out of the classroom. I shoved my notebook in my bag and ran directly to the office.

Mrs Stobo looked up when I poked my head in the doorway.

"Hello, Ruby. What do you need, honey?"

This habit of calling people 'honey' never ceases to amaze me. Back home, honey is something criminals are forced to eat in prison.

"I'm looking for my hat. I was wondering if anyone had handed it in to Lost Property?"

"When, from the trip just now?"

I nodded.

"No, I'm afraid nothing's been handed in."

"Oh." *Never mind*, I told myself. *There's still time. There's still time. There's still time...*

Mrs Stobo smiled kindly. "Ruby, you know, you look good without a hat. You should consider not wearing one all the time. Perhaps just when it's cold?"

Not wear a hat? How would that work? That was what I was thinking, but all I said was, "Thanks for the tip. I'll take it on board." I'd heard adults say this when they really meant, "I wouldn't do that in a hundred million trillion years, not even if you paid me all the bronze ingots in the world," but I didn't want to be rude.

I walked home. My dad would already have picked up Carl when he got out of school half an hour ago, and they didn't wait around for me any more now that the weather was getting colder. By the time I got in, my mum was home from work. She was in the kitchen, stirring something in the cauldron.

"Hi, Slimeball."

"Hi Mum." I scurried through to the living room in the hope that she wouldn't see me without my hat.

"Whoah, wait right there," she said.

I stopped. She'd seen me. It would now be necessary to implement Operation Maternal Deception.

"Where's your hat?" she asked, eyebrows raised.

"Oh, it's in my bag," I said, in what I hoped was a casual tone.

"Why aren't you wearing it?" I had to be careful; my mum could sniff out a lie at a hundred giant's paces.

"Because no one else wears a fleece hat all the time, and I'm trying to fit in," I replied. I knew this argument would get to her.

"Oh. OK. I just wanted to make sure you hadn't lost it."

"Lost it?" I tried to appear offended. "No, it's right

here in my bag, where I said it was. Do you want me to show you? Or do you actually *trust* me for once?"

I was taking a big risk here that she'd call my bluff.

"No, that's OK; of course I trust you," she said quickly, looking a little flustered.

My ploy had worked. I knew exactly which of my mum's buttons to push.

"Just make sure you have it when I do the inventory on Monday," she added, returning to her cooking.

I guess my bluff had only been partially effective. But at least it had bought me a bit more time.

I was about to head to my bedroom, when I saw something small and fluffy scamper across the kitchen floor. It disappeared through the cat flap with a wave of its bushy tail.

"Was that a—"

"Squirrel? Yes," Mum said, and then tasted what she was cooking.

"But what..."

She looked up again. "Oh, it's Vronsky."

"What? How is that possible?"

"Being here in the Ord World does something funny to his chemical make-up, confuses it somehow. That's why he's having trouble... adjusting."

"So he's not just a dog?"

"That's what we thought at first, but it hasn't stayed that way. I think it might have something to do with changes in air pressure, but I'm not sure."

"Huh." Poor Vronksy, he was having just as bad a time of it as I was.

"Hey, could you taste this and tell me what you think?" Mum held her hand beneath the spoon to catch the drips as I took a taste.

"Mmm. It's good. But I think it needs more arsenic."

"Yeah, that's what I was thinking, too. Thanks."

I couldn't tell whether she was making a soup, a stew or a sauce. "Is this dinner?" I asked. My mum didn't usually start cooking so early; she normally bunged a few ingredients in the cauldron twenty minutes before it was time to eat, or popped some frozen toad fillets in the oven. (That was back in Hexadonia, of course; here, we had to make do with something called chicken nuggets instead. Gross.)

She nodded.

"Have we ever had that before?"

"No. I'm trying a new recipe. It's for work."

As we were talking, the squirrel reappeared through the cat flap, and stopped to lap up a saucer of milk. Spotting me, it climbed up my leg and nudged my hand happily.

"Hey, Vronsk. Nice tail." He curled his bushy tail into a question mark and tickled my nose.

"Where's Dad?" I asked, trying not to sneeze.

"He's in the bathroom, practising on your brother."

"Practising what?"

"Go see." She smiled.

I dumped my stuff in my room and then gingerly

approached the bathroom door. Knocking, I heard my dad's voice call, "Come on in; it's open."

I pushed the door open and was taken aback by the sight that greeted me. My brother was seated on the closed toilet lid with one of those plastic hair-cutting sheets draped round his shoulders. He appeared to have spikes coming out of his head, but on closer inspection it turned out that his slicked hair was twisted into elaborate shapes. There must have been about a litre of gel in it.

"What the—"

"Hi, Slimeball." My dad was wearing rubber gloves, and looked like a sculptor, hard at work on my brother's hair.

"What are you doing?"

"I'm trying out some new styles. For work." His tongue poked out in concentration.

"Do they usually ask the floor sweeper to come up with new hairstyles?"

Dad stopped what he was doing and looked at me. I could tell that a lecture was forming in his head.

"How do you think Vidal Sassoon got his start?"

"Who's that?" asked Carl.

"Only one of the world's most famous hair stylists. He didn't wait around for someone to ask him to invent new styles. He grabbed the gremlin by the horns and went for it."

"Oh. OK." Carl was wriggling around impatiently. "Can I see the back, Dad?"

My dad handed him a small mirror, and he looked into

it with the big mirror behind him. The three-inch spikes covered his whole head.

I was impressed.

"You look like a cross between a hairbrush and a demented hedgehog."

Carl grinned. "Cool!"

The next day, I got to school early and ran straight to the office.

"Has anyone turned in my fleece hat?" I asked Mrs Stobo, trying not to sound as eager as I actually was.

"No," she laughed, "not between the end of school yesterday and the beginning of school today. Not many people are here yet. Give it a bit of time, dear."

I walked slowly to class. I didn't even try to concentrate on my lessons; all I could think about was the hat. At break time, I ran back to the office.

"Has anyone—"

Mrs Stobo shook her head. "Sorry, honey."

The hours crawled by until lunch. We had a spelling test, which I messed up because I'd lost my lucky quill ages ago and I just couldn't concentrate. I kept thinking about the spelling tests we had back home, which were completely different: we had to demonstrate our knowledge of spells and incantations. I remembered the Spelling Bee we had every year, where pupils would be assigned spells in a competition, and you'd have to cast them right there in front of everyone. For example, the judge might say: "Invisibility Spell, 50% potency." That's the spell you use if you want just the right or left half of your body to be visible. It's for when you really want to freak someone out. Or they might give you the Operatic Spell, which makes the victim sing at the top of their lungs every time they open their mouth. It's great for when you know your enemy will be going to the library. Or the Mushy Toes Spell. That one's self-explanatory.

But of course, now there were no more Spelling Bees, because there were no more spells. I liked to recite spells in my head to keep them fresh in my mind, but some of them were already beginning to fade, and that frightened me. I had to get my magic back, and soon.

When the lunch bell rang, I sprang out of class and sprinted to the office to check with Mrs Stobo again.

"Has—"

"No. Still no hat. Sorry, dear."

I could hardly eat anything at lunch. I sat by myself at a big, otherwise empty table and stared at my food. I could see the Purple Mafia sitting and whispering at 'their' table. Georgia's minions were pointing at me and giggling. Georgia was listening to what they were saying, but she wasn't laughing. She looked over at me now and again, seemingly more out of curiosity than anything else. I was probably like a zoo animal to her, something weird and unusual to stare at when she felt like it.

At one point, she seemed to smile at me, but I turned away without responding. It was probably a trick, or she was just taunting me. I couldn't believe I was going to have to go her party, at her actual *house*. I spent the rest of lunchtime thinking about all the ways that she could be mean to me when I was on her home turf. I would be at her mercy.

Lunch ended, and we had another test. Weeks without a single assessment, and then two in one day! It was a maths test, on angles. I didn't even get the pentangle question right, and that should have been a no-brainer. We were just handing in our papers when I saw Mrs Stobo appear in the doorway of the classroom. She motioned for me to come over and ushered me into the hall. "Someone's handed in a ski hat. I thought you'd like to know."

My hat! I knew it would turn up!

"Here you go," she said, smiling as she handed me a black hat.

I was so excited, I could hardly breathe. I turned the hat over, but something didn't feel quite right. On closer inspection, I saw that this hat had a sports brand logo sewn into the side. My hat didn't have a brand on it, only the words 'Made in China' on the inside. In other words, this wasn't my hat. Mum wouldn't fail to notice this on inspection day, and the deal would be off.

I couldn't remember feeling this disappointed since I found out we'd have to leave Hexadonia. I slowly handed the hat back to Mrs Stobo, shaking my head. I couldn't speak. I turned and walked back into the classroom.

I felt all eyes on me as I slipped back behind my desk, determined not to cry.

Out of the corner of my eye, I noticed Georgia looking at me again from across the room. When she saw that I was watching her, she quickly looked away.

CHAPTER 14

Halloween had finally arrived. My parents were preparing to take Carl out guising. I discovered that 'guising' comes from the word 'disguise'. Carl was going as a zombie; my mum had insisted that he not go as anything too scary to Ords. My parents had decided to 'dress up' too, as in wear their old work clothes. Mum wore her long black hair loose, and if you looked hard you could see her green roots, which she normally tried to cover up with hair dye. Her tall pointed hat had a small brim (not one of those big, floppy brims you see on fake witch costumes, which are *so* unrealistic), and her long black gown was cinched at the waist. My dad wore a knee-length midnight blue cloak with high boots, and a small pointy blue hat with gold embroidery running up the sides. They both carried their collapsible broomsticks in holsters by their side.

With my parents in their old clothes and me in my Sorcery Academy uniform, it felt a little like the good old days. I sighed wistfully.

I wished I didn't have to go to Georgia's party. Why were my parents forcing me to do this?

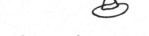

I waited until the last minute to leave, and just as I was about to walk out the door, the bell rang.

"I'll get it!" Carl squealed.

A couple of costumed kids stood on the porch.

"OK, let's see what you've got," Carl said suddenly business-like, crossing his arms.

The rest of us crowded into the doorway to observe the strange customs of the natives.

A small child wearing a crooked vampire mask asked, "Why did the headless horseman work really hard?"

Carl pretended to think for a moment. Finally he said, "I don't know. Why *did* the headless horseman work really hard?"

"So he could get ahead! A head – get it?"

"Ahhh, good one." Dad nodded his approval.

"My turn," said the other child, who was wearing a 'witch' costume that her mother had clearly picked up for half price somewhere. "What does Godzilla have for his tea?"

"I don't know." Carl played along. "What *does* Godzilla have for his tea?"

"Traffic jam sandwiches!" the girl said, clearly for the hundredth time that evening. She really needed to work on her delivery.

Nonetheless, my brother and parents made a show of falling about laughing. "Very good!" Mum cried. "I think you've both earned your treat."

Carl held out a large salad bowl filled with wriggling millipedes. "Help yourselves," he said. "They're fresh from the garden. They tickle going down."

The children hesitated, and then gingerly chose one each.

"Thank you," they said weakly.

"You're welcome," my mum said. "Happy Halloween!"

I was glad I wasn't going to be sticking around to witness many more of these little performances, and I'm not just talking about the guisers.

"I'm off now," I said as I headed out.

My mum tried to tweak my nose, but I brushed her off gruffly. I wasn't in the mood for sentimental mushiness. I was about to face a party full of monsters. And not the good kind.

"Have a nice time," she said.

"Yes, and remember, back by nine," Dad added.

"Oh, I'll be back sooner than that," I said. "I'm sure it'll be really boring."

I slammed the door and walked out into the night. The clocks had gone back an hour a few days earlier, and it was already dark. I was glad that Daylight Saving Time was so straightforward here. Back home, we had Island Summer Time, which involved turning the clocks forward 42½ minutes for 17 days, and then back 3 hours and 56 minutes for two days, and then forward again by 36 seconds for 8 hours and 9 minutes. Whenever I heard Ords complain about the clocks going back, I marvelled at how easy they had it.

As I made my way down the street, I saw groups of

children, sometimes accompanied by a parent or two, dressed as zombies and ghosts (why do Ords think that ghosts are white? And what's with the sheets? Everyone knows that only bed phantoms wear sheets, not ghosts). I also saw a lot of very fake-looking witches, but they didn't fool me. At one point, though, as I bent down behind a wall to tie one of my trainer laces, I noticed three particularly realistic 'witches' walk past me. Their costumes were so authentic-looking that I was wondering where they had bought them, when I heard them croak to each other in low voices.

"Do you think we'll see any of 'em tonight?" one of them rasped.

"Of course," said another. "Have you ever known any witches to stay home on Halloween?"

All three of them cackled.

"Have you worked out which place is theirs?" asked the third one.

"I think it's one of those over there." The second 'witch' pointed back towards the direction I'd just come from.

It sounded like the first one said, "Well, it won't be long now," but I can't be sure, because they had walked too far away by then.

Their conversation struck me as a bit creepy, but I'd learned that Ords could be very strange, and I didn't have time to stop and think too much about it. I was really late by now, so I hurried towards Georgia's house, arriving at her front door ten minutes later.

The place was huge; it must have been twice the size of our house. I knocked on the large wooden door and Georgia's brother Logan answered. He was dressed as a vampire and was holding a bowl of miniature chocolate bars.

"Hi, Ruby!" He looked pleased to see me.

"Hi, Logan." I smiled.

"Come in," he said. "I wasn't sure if it was guisers or someone for the party." He held out the bowl of chocolate bars. "Want one?"

"No thanks," I said politely, trying not to show my revulsion.

"Georgia's supposed to be answering the door, but she's in the garage fetching more fizzy juice. I'll show you round."

Good. The longer I could stay out of her way the better.

"Where are your mum and dad?" I asked.

"They're hiding out in the study."

"Oh. OK." Just great. No adults to stop any Purple Mafia antics.

"The food's through there." He pointed to the large kitchen. "People are playing games in there," he continued, leading me past what looked like a dining room. "Some are out on the patio, too. We've got those outdoor heaters, so it shouldn't be too cold. Make yourself at home."

"Thanks."

He padded off, and I was left on my own. Checking to make sure the coast was clear, I wandered into the living room, eager to see how rich people lived in the Ordinary World. Back home, we had been relatively well off, but here we seemed to have less than other kids' families, or at least most of the kids in my school. That was another hard thing about coming here, on top of everything else.

Sure enough, the Finnegans' living room was as opulent as the rest of the house. The wooden floor was polished to a high shine and there was a big fireplace in the middle of the far wall with a collection of crystal vases displayed on the mantelpiece, along with several framed photographs. It was interesting to see what kinds of things were important to Ords. Back in Hexadonia, there would have been photos of brooms, of course, and of hats – every family had their own collection, which was handed down from generation to generation. Some things, I noticed, were the same in both places: there were lots of photos of cats here, just as there would have been back home, and pictures of family members and holidays. One photo in particular caught my eye: it must have been of Georgia and Logan when they were much younger. A little blonde girl sat holding a baby on her knee. They looked to be perched on a balcony high above a misty valley. There was something kind of compelling about the scene, something almost familiar – but I couldn't put my finger on what it was.

I figured I'd better join the rest of the party before I got caught snooping around. I walked into the dining room, and saw kids playing that game where you try to take bites out of a dead rat hanging on a string – only, instead of a rat, the Ords use a donut.

Now, I don't like to toot my own horn, but I happen to be an expert at this particular game. We used to play it every Halloween back home, and I would always win. The best part was that the winner got to finish off the rest of the rat. Delicious.

I figured that a donut hanging from a string couldn't be that different from a rodent, and I was right, except for the disgusting taste. How Ords eat those things, I will never know. I went up to a donut, put my hands behind my back in a professional manner, and just went for it. I managed to eat the thing in three seconds flat. On either side of me, a Grim Reaper and a vampire were still banging their noses against their donuts by the time I had finished mine. I didn't even break a sweat.

I was about to head to the kitchen for something to take the horrible donut taste out of my mouth, when someone dressed in a purple ghost costume suddenly appeared.

"RUBY?" she said in a very loud voice. "IS THAT YOU?"

"Yes," I replied hesitantly, not sure whether I was supposed to recognise them.

"It's Kirsty," said the purple ghost.

"Uh-huh," I replied, glancing round to see if there was an escape route nearby.

"I like your costume." She looked me up and down.

"Oh, it's just my old school—" I started to say, but then caught myself.

"Your what?"

"It's very old-school," I said. "Very old-fashioned. Not like the witch costumes you see nowadays. It was handed down to me by my... grandmother." I guess I didn't need to embellish my lie with so much detail, but I was a little nervous. I couldn't understand why Kirsty, one of the Purple Mafia, was deigning to talk to me. Could it be that I was finally beginning to fit in?

"Oh, yes, I guess it is a bit old-fashioned." She seemed to be admiring the detailing on my collar. "How very... charming."

"Thanks," I said.

"Well, RUBY," Kirsty said in a booming voice, "it's great to see you, RUBY." She was nearly shouting now.

Everyone in the room was doing that thing where you look at someone while trying to appear as though you're not looking at them. I wasn't surprised that so many people were staring at us, considering how loudly Kirsty had been talking.

Kirsty motioned to Rachel, the other Purple Mafia minion, who had been standing a few metres away. She, too, was dressed as a purple ghost.

"Rachel," Kirsty said, "did you know Ruby was here?"

"No, I didn't," Rachel replied, though I couldn't imagine how this could be true, given that Kirsty had just shouted my name loudly enough for the whole of Edinburgh to hear. "Hi, Ruby."

"Er, hi." I couldn't get over how much attention the

Purple Mafia were showing me. Had they changed, or had I?

"Ruby, why don't you come out to the back garden?" Rachel suggested. "The Finnegans' garden is lovely."

Swept away by the fact that these girls were actually talking to me for once, I figured I'd go wherever they wanted, even if their sudden interest in the Finnegans' flowerbeds was a bit odd.

"COME THIS WAY, RUBY," Rachel shouted as we walked outside, where about a dozen of my classmates were gathered in small groups, chatting and laughing. As we arrived, loads of others crowded through the patio doors. It was as though they had been waiting to see something, and now the time had arrived.

As soon as we were outside, I noticed that Kirsty had hung back, and now she was talking into what looked like a mobile phone, but which turned out to be a walkie-talkie. There were so many people in the way that I couldn't really hear what she was saying, but I distinctly heard the words "Operation H_2O."

I turned to Rachel. "I just heard Kirsty talking about an operation. Is everything OK?"

Rachel froze, and then arranged her face into a tight smile. "An operation? Oh, yes, it's her grandfather. He has to have an operation. For... for a new hip. Yeah, that's it. Kirsty was just wishing him well." Rachel looked very pleased with herself, for some reason.

"A new hip? Oh, that sounds painful." The whole

world of surgery, and Ord medicine generally, was a completely new concept for me. I was used to going to the witch doctor, who knew all sorts of specialist charms and incantations to fix virtually any physical ailment under the sun (and under the moon, too). If you had something really serious, you went to hospital, where witch surgeons danced around you until you were better. The good ones were expensive, but they got the job done at the first appointment. You didn't want to go to one of those cut-rate surgeons, who would do a half-hearted healing dance while checking w-mail on his phone, and then have to go see another witch surgeon to undo the damage caused by the first one.

When I snapped out of my daydream of dancing doctors, I noticed that lots of kids were whispering and pointing at me. Georgia was still nowhere to be seen.

Something was definitely off.

The Purples suddenly appeared, shuffling and giggling, clearly hiding something behind their backs. I had a bad feeling in my stomach as suddenly everyone fell silent. There was a brief moment of silence before Georgia's lieutenant, Rachel, nodded her head twice.

"Ready!" she shouted. Before I could react, she yelled "FIRE!"

Next, everything seemed to happen in slow motion. Rachel and several others whipped out water guns and balloons. I saw Georgia, who was dressed as a purple Bride of Frankenstein, run out onto the patio, and yell, "NO!"

But it was too late.

Water from the guns hit me first. It saturated my clothes, and was wet and cold and horrible. The worst was still to come, though.

Seconds later, water balloons exploded in my face. The impact sent me to my knees. I tried to shield myself as the next hideous blast drenched me. More jets of water, more awful, soaking balloons.

Then the biggest wave of all forced me to the ground.

And then there was darkness.

CHAPTER 15

When I came to, I wasn't sure where I was at first. The last thing I remembered was being in Georgia's back garden; the rest was a bit fuzzy. But I soon realised that I wasn't at the party any more. I was lying in my own bed.

My mum was hovering over me anxiously. "She's awake!" she called out, and a minute later my dad appeared.

"What happened?" I said groggily.

"It's all right, Slimeball," he said gently. "At the Halloween party last night—"

"Last night? It's the next day already?"

"Yes, you've slept quite a bit. You were in a state of shock after the water-spraying incident. You'll probably need to sleep some more."

"WATER?" I shrieked. Now it was beginning to come back to me. The whole hideous, soggy wetness of it all.

"It's OK," Mum said in her most soothing voice. "It was just a bit of Halloween hijinks. You're home and dry now."

Just a bit of Halloween hijinks?

"It was Georgia Finnegan and her evil purple minions," I said angrily. "They planned the whole thing. It was like a military operation. They even used *walkie-talkies*. Who uses walkie-talkies? And that's what Kirsty meant by 'Operation H_2O' – it wasn't her grandfather's hip! And that's why the Purples were so friendly to me, and why they kept saying my name so loudly, to alert the others—"

My parents looked at each other with concern. "She's delirious," Dad whispered.

"I'm afraid so," agreed my mother.

"Why don't you just rest a little longer?" Mum tucked the duvet up under my chin. The two of them gave me sympathetic smiles before slipping out of the room.

I dozed on and off for the rest of the day. At dinner time Mum tried to get me to eat something, but I had no appetite. All I wanted to do was close my eyes. I knew I should never have gone to that party. Like they would actually want to be friends with me! I felt so stupid. I hated my life here. I wanted to go home. I wanted my magic back.

When I woke again, it was morning. Mum was in my bedroom, pulling open the curtains.

"Hey, Sleepyhead," she said in a sing-song voice, "I think you've slept enough for the next year. It's time for school."

School? Was she kidding? There was no way I was going to school, not after what had happened.

"But I can't go to school!" I cried.

"Why not?"

"Because... Because, I'm... sick!" I said triumphantly.

"Sick?" She gave me a sceptical smile.

I coughed. "Yes, sick. See?" I coughed again, for good measure.

I could tell by the look in my mother's eyes that she didn't believe me, but she simply said, "OK. I'll call the school office. But you're going to be on your own today. Your dad and I both have to work."

Success! I tried not to grin. "That's no problem. I can look after myself."

"I'll come home early to see how you're getting on."

"Not necessary, but be my guest."

My dad came in to say goodbye on his way to take Carl to school.

"Do you want me to bring home some deep conditioning treatment from the shop?"

"I suppose." I would have to do something different with my hair now that I didn't have a hat. Maybe I could slick it back with conditioner and a bit of grease.

"How are you feeling?" asked Carl, with uncharacteristic sympathy.

I attempted a pathetic cough. "Not great."

Carl turned to my father. "I told you she's not sick! She's just faking it to get off school!"

What a two-faced, tiny-headed backstabber.

"Your sister isn't feeling well," Dad said firmly, bustling him out of the room.

Carl turned back to look at me just as the door was closing, and I stuck my tongue out at him. As he walked through the door, Dad said, "Don't open the door to any strangers. Do you understand, Ruby?"

I nodded. Boy, my dad could be paranoid sometimes. What did he think was going to happen? That someone would kidnap me and demand a ransom? Well, they'd be picking the wrong house if they did. We barely had enough money to make ends meet. My parents would probably just say to the kidnapper, "Go ahead and take her. She's yours."

When everybody had left the house, I got up. I had just spent the last two days in bed, and couldn't stand being cooped up in my room any longer. I went to the kitchen and made myself a cup of twig tea and some toast. My mother had thoughtfully left a dish of snails on the table, which I gulped down greedily.

I assessed my situation. Today was the 2nd of November, the day of the big inspection. When my mother got home from work this evening, she would discover that I'd lost my fleece hat, and she wouldn't let us go to Arthur's Seat on Bonfire Night, meaning that I'd never be able to get my magic back. I was condemned to live here forever with these horrible, mean people in this strange world where there was still so much I didn't understand. I couldn't pretend to be sick for ever; soon, I'd have to go back to school, where most of the people there disliked me enough to come up with an epic plan to humiliate me in public. Things would only get worse, not better.

I moped about the house. I couldn't bring myself to get dressed. After a while, I thought I'd watch some television. I flicked through the channels, but every programme was either a cooking show or a DIY show. Why were Ords so obsessed with this stuff? Since there was nothing else on, I tried watching a few programmes for a while to see if I could figure out why they were so popular.

Six hours later, I was still watching. I saw people who called themselves 'chefs' commit atrocities that they called 'cooking', but the things they made turned my stomach: stuff like vanilla sponge, which at first sounded pretty good, until I saw that it wasn't made with actual sponges. I also learned a lot of home decorating tips for Ord dwellings, but I couldn't believe the colours they liked to paint their walls – like, white! Or sometimes, girls in this stupid world actually chose to paint their bedrooms pink, of their own free will. Disgusting.

I looked up at the clock on the mantelpiece and saw that school would be getting out soon. I realised that I hadn't eaten anything since breakfast, so I went to the kitchen to make myself a sandwitch. They have something quite similar here called 'sandwiches', but those have the filling on the *inside*, which doesn't make sense to me.

As I was eating, I heard a loud thud come from the living room. Going to investigate, I saw a squirrel – that is, Vronsky – nudging Jeremy across the carpet. I stared in disbelief as he gave one final push, and Jeremy bumped up against the front door.

"Ahem," said Jeremy.

I looked down.

"Would you mind?" he asked.

"I don't think you should go out today," I replied.

"Why not?"

"Because you've been known to cause trouble."

"Trouble? *Moi?*"

I raised an eyebrow.

"OK. Up to you. I'll just sit here and ask until you let me out. Your choice."

"You can ask all you want, but I'm not letting you out." I turned to go back to my sandwitch.

"Let me out."

I ignored him.

"Let me out."

"Not listening." I put my hands over my ears.

"Let me out let me out let me out let me out let me out let me—"

"OK, you win." I opened the door and kicked him outside. Sometimes he could be even more annoying than Carl, and that was saying something.

Jeremy rolled onto the doorstep and came to a stop next to a carved Halloween pumpkin that was still sitting on the porch. "Hey good lookin'," I heard him say as I shut the door. "You come here often?"

I was just walking back into the kitchen when the doorbell rang. I wasn't supposed to answer it but figured that it must be Jeremy wanting to come back in again anyway, so I ignored it and carried on walking, but then it rang again. I wondered how Jeremy had managed to reach the bell by himself. Carrying my sandwitch, I went back to the door and opened it, saying, "I told you this wasn't a good idea—"

I stopped suddenly. It wasn't Jeremy. It was Georgia, in her school uniform. I couldn't believe it. She had the nerve to show up here after what she'd done? I slammed the door in her face.

She knocked on the door again. "Ruby, open up!"

"Go away!"

"I've come to apologise."

Yeah, right. A likely story.

"Please let me in," Georgia pleaded.

I remained silent. I wasn't falling for her tricks again.

"Ruby. I know about you."

I couldn't keep quiet any longer (and being behind a door made me feel just a little bit braver). "You know about me? Well, I know about you, too. You're a mean, two-faced, horrible person who preys on people's weaknesses; that's what you are!"

"Ruby."

I didn't answer this time.

"Ruby," she said again. "I know you're a witch."

My sandwitch fell to the floor.

"No, I'm not," I said, after a pause. I guess I panicked.

"Come on. You don't have to pretend with me."

"Don't be ridiculous. What makes you think I'm a witch?" I said indignantly, as though my anger somehow proved I wasn't one.

There was silence. It lasted so long that I thought maybe Georgia had left, but then I heard her voice again, quieter this time.

"Ruby, I know you're a witch… because I'm a witch, too."

CHAPTER 16

I stood in front of the door in a state of shock. Finally I heard myself say, "You're a *witch*?"

"Well, I used to be a witch. I guess I'm not any more. Though my mum always says, 'You can take the witch out of Hexadonia but you can't take Hexadonia out of the witch.' I don't know if that makes any sense to you."

Make any sense to me? It was what my mum always said, too. I opened the door.

"Hi," Georgia said meekly. She somehow looked smaller without her minions by her side.

"Hi," I said.

"Can I come in?"

I stood back and led her into the living room, where she sat down on the sofa nervously.

"Would you like something to drink?" I asked, as my mum had taught me. "Juice? Some tea?"

Georgia smiled. "Tea would be great, if it's no trouble."

"Sure. Regular? Or we have twig, or some dried beetles' brains..."

"Regular's fine. I've been here a long time now."

I sat on the sofa opposite her. "You moved here from Hexadonia? When?"

"I was six, and Logan was just a toddler. He doesn't remember anything about our old life. He's fascinated by the whole thing, though."

That would explain why he'd glommed on to Carl, and why he seemed to love everything about our family when he came over for dinner. Even in Hexadonia, where we had lots of friends, no one loved *everything* about our family.

"Why did you guys move?" I asked.

"You know, I'm not really sure. My mum and dad both worked for the Aerozoom Broom Corporation—"

"Hey, so did my parents!" I wondered whether they had known each other.

"That was pretty much the only place to work if you were in the aviation industry, wasn't it?"

"Yeah, I guess so."

"My parents just weren't happy there," said Georgia. "I never did find out why. But they decided to move here to start over."

"Yeah, so did mine, only they did it all really suddenly." Then I remembered the tea. "I'll be back in a minute."

As I went into the kitchen, my mind reeled. I couldn't process what Georgia had told me. How was it possible that she was a witch? How could I not even have had an inkling? That must be why I'd noticed her staring at me so often – she must have worked out that I was a witch pretty early on.

I brought the tea through to the living room and

poured some out for both of us.

"So," she said, settling into her seat, "I guess I should explain everything, but first I want to say sorry for Kirsty and Rachel. What they did at my party, I mean. I tried to stop them, but I guess that doesn't matter."

I had a vague memory of hearing Georgia's voice shouting "NO!" just before the attack. I looked down at my tea. "Yeah, it wasn't exactly the best Halloween party I've ever been to."

There was an awkward silence. So many questions were whizzing through my head, and there were still some things I couldn't work out. "How did you know I was a witch?"

Georgia played with the handle of her mug awkwardly. "Remember on your first day, when you were talking about pentangles? That's what made me suspect, but I wasn't certain. Then, when I saw you trying to make a potion in the chemistry class at the high school, my suspicion grew stronger. But it was only when I saw you at the party dressed in your Academy uniform that I knew for sure. And of course, I know a real witch's hat when I see one. Plus, you wear a cape to school. It's kind of a giveaway." She smiled.

"But why did you organise the drenching? That was so cruel."

Georgia looked embarrassed and took a sip of her tea, as though she were putting off something she didn't want to say. "Kirsty and Rachel planned it all. I asked them not to, but they did it anyway."

This didn't make sense. The Purple Mafia seemed to hang on Georgia's every word. "I don't understand. Why did you have to play along? They're your friends; they do whatever you tell them, don't they?"

She paused. "They're not really my friends."

"I don't get it." The next thing I said in a very quiet voice; it was the thing I had the most trouble understanding. "Why have you been so horrible to me?"

Georgia looked down and didn't say anything for the longest time. Finally she said, "At first I found it really hard to fit in here, but when I was mean to people, they stopped and listened. After a while being horrible seemed the only way I'd get people to like me."

I was confused. "How could being horrible make people like you?"

"It doesn't," she said, almost in a whisper. "They don't like me. They're afraid of me. Those are two very different things."

I sat there stunned. Before I could say anything, I heard a loud clattering noise coming from the kitchen. There were sounds of scuffing and snorting, and they seemed to be coming closer.

Two seconds later, a pig burst into the living room.

"Is that your familiar?" Georgia said, as the pig snorted and attempted to rub its back against my leg.

"No..." I began, but the pig jumped clumsily into my lap. "Er, I think it is."

"Vronsky?" I cried.

The pig began to purr.

"Our familiar keeps shape shifting too," Georgia said. "But we've been here a while now, so she doesn't transform that often. She's a chicken just now. The cleaning bills are through the roof."

"Huh," I said, as the pig began licking its hooves.

Georgia stood up. "I'm really sorry, but I have to go. My mum will kill me if I'm not home soon. I just wanted to explain things, to say sorry. And I suppose, to let you know that you're not on your own. I promise to stop being mean to you. I'd really like to be friends, but I'll understand if you never want to speak to me again." She fiddled with her bag strap.

I thought for a second, but the choice seemed pretty easy: either continue being completely alone, or try to make friends with the one person who might possibly understand me.

"I'll speak to you," I said. "I may not speak to Kirsty and Rachel, but I'll speak to you."

"I may not speak to them, either," Georgia said.

She turned to leave, and was almost out the door when she stopped and pulled something from her bag.

"Oh, I almost forgot. I wanted to give this back to you. Rachel had it."

She handed me a soft, black object. I stared at it for a moment before realising what it was.

It was my fleece hat.

CHAPTER 17

I must have stood holding the hat for a good two minutes. I turned it over and over in my hands to make sure it was actually mine. It was – there was no doubt about it.

It was almost too much to take in. Georgia a witch, and a lot more vulnerable than I could ever have imagined. And I had my hat back! This meant I would pass my mum's inspection, and she would have to take me to Arthur's Seat on Bonfire Night, and I might actually get my magic back...

At that moment, the front door opened. It was my mum.

"How are you doing?" she asked. She was wearing her Burger Barn uniform, which consisted of a matching orange and brown top and trousers and, of course, the paper hat, which she wore pinned to her hair at a jaunty angle. She looked unusually perky.

"Fine," I said, trying not to look too guilty.

"Yes, you're looking rather better than when I left you this morning," she said with a twinkle in her eye.

"Hmmm," I agreed. "It's amazing what a bit of rest can do."

"Isn't it just." She put her handbag down and came over to me. "Now Slimeball," she said gently; I could tell she was gearing up for a big speech. "I know this has been really hard for you, but you're going to have to go back to school tomorrow. You can't just—"

"That's no problem."

"Don't interrupt me. You can't just stay off school because you don't feel like—"

"I said it's no problem. I'm happy to go back to school."

My mum seemed surprised. "You are?"

"Sure."

"Oh. OK." She looked slightly relieved, as if she'd been expecting an argument.

"And Mum – can we do the inspection now?"

She hesitated. "Do we have to? I have something to tell you guys."

"Yes. I want to do it RIGHT NOW." There was no way I was going to risk losing my hat again.

"OK, then," she said distractedly. "Let's do this. Then I want to tell you something."

"Sure, sure," I pulled her upstairs and into my room, "but before we start, I want to tell *you* something. I would like you to note that I have my hat right here. In case you were wondering."

"Uh. OK." Mum looked at me oddly.

She began searching around my room, picking up random objects.

"Where's your earthworm hair clip?" she asked.

"Here," I said triumphantly, grabbing the clip from my bedside table.

Then she started looking through my drawers. She held up a sock with a bat on it. "Where's the mate to this?"

I reached behind my wardrobe and pulled out the other sock. Before my mum could speak, I added, "You didn't say anything about having to be tidy. All I had to do was not lose things."

She considered this and then nodded. "Fair enough."

She began snooping around my bookshelf. "Where's your maggot lip balm? It used to be on one of these shelves."

"Not any more," I said, whipping the lip balm out of my trouser pocket. "Wouldn't want chapped lips now, would I?"

Mum smiled. "OK, you've passed the test."

I blinked. "What, that was it?"

"Yes, that was it. I hereby declare you have won the wager," she said, as though she wanted to hurry things.

"DOES THAT MEAN WE CAN GO TO ARTHUR'S SEAT FOR BONFIRE NIGHT?" I jumped onto my bed in excitement.

"Lower your voice. Yes, it does. And get down!"

I wanted to do a triple backflip, I was so happy. But I restrained myself.

"Listen, Ruby," Mum said suddenly, "is your dad home?"

"No."

"Because I've got some news. Some wonderful news."

Now that I wasn't so focused on passing the inspection, I saw that she was beaming.

"What is it?"

"I want to wait until your father and brother are home to tell everyone."

As if on cue, we heard them come through the front door. I ran downstairs into the kitchen, Mum following behind me. Dad was looking a bit bewildered by Vronsky's new piggy form, and Carl was already sitting at the kitchen table, stuffing his face with dried wasps.

"OK, everyone's here," I said to Mum, "so tell us."

"Tell us what?" Carl asked around a mouthful of wings and antennae.

"I got a promotion at work!" Mum practically shouted.

"That's fantastic!" Dad cried, lifting her up in the air and giving her a big tweak on the nose. Vronksy squealed excitedly.

"They liked my new sauce recipe," she said. "They're going to start putting it on the burgers next week. They said it showed good initiative, and they've made me Assistant Manager!"

"Yippee!" Carl cried. "So does this mean we'll have more money?"

"Yes," Mum told him. "Not a huge amount, but a bit more. Things won't be quite so tight."

"So I'll be able to get a new pair of trainers?" Carl said.

"You'll be able to get a new pair of trainers," Mum confirmed happily.

"We'll have to go out and celebrate." Dad turned to Mum. "Where shall we go?"

"Anywhere. Surprise me."

My dad took my mum at her word and really surprised her by shepherding us all to Burger Barn. Mum was a good sport about it though, and wore her paper hat with pride.

I was happy, too, because in three days I might have my magic back. Three days! Fizzing with excitement, I began crossing off the days on a calendar on my wall.

When I saw Georgia again at school over the next couple of days, she wasn't mean, and she actually talked to me, even sitting with me in lessons and at lunch instead of with Kirsty and Rachel. She still wore a lot of purple accessories ("What can I say?" She shrugged. "I like purple."), but she wore other colours, too. I stopped sitting alone at break times, because when they saw Georgia taking an interest, other people started talking to me, too. We had an important secret that we shared, and that no one else knew. I didn't feel so alone any more. I didn't go so far as to join Girl Guides or the cricket team (a pale imitation of cockroach as far as I'm concerned), but it was still progress.

I still wore my ski hat to school, but I experimented

with other hats, too; my mum treated me to a couple of new ones. Apparently my old one smelled. I didn't understand why that was a bad thing, but I did need more hats now that my dad had roped me into being a guinea pig for his hair sculptures. He really pulled out all the stops on the designs he was working on, which he planned to roll out for special occasions: for Bonfire Night he practised an effigy of Guy Fawkes on my head, and he experimented with special styles for other upcoming holidays, like Valentine's Day (a big heart) and Christmas (a fir tree complete with baubles) – all plastered on top of my head with a litre of hair gel. His hard work paid off, because by the end of the week he got a promotion too, to trainee hair stylist. We went to Burger Barn again to celebrate, and we could taste my mum's special sauce on the burgers.

With all this going on in the space of just a few days, I didn't have a lot of time to dwell on the thought of Bonfire Night, but in the back of my mind, it was always there: the possibility of going home and, more than anything else, getting my magic back. But just occasionally, when I let my mind wander, it seemed that now I was starting to settle in at school and learn more about the strange ways of the Ords, I was becoming less certain about where home really was.

There was one weird thing, though. I kept seeing those three women in the massive woolly hats around my neighbourhood. I realised why they looked familiar.

They reminded me of the guard witches at my parents' work, who I remembered seeing when we went on a school trip. They used to circle the company headquarters on the lookout for – I don't know – thieves, I guess, or spies (broom manufacturing is a cut-throat business), and you could sometimes hear them cackling from way up high. It didn't make sense that they'd be here in the Ord World, though. Once, when I was coming home from school, I even thought I saw them in our front garden, but when they saw me approaching, they seemed to scurry away. I told myself that the anticipation of waiting for Bonfire Night was probably getting to me and making me imagine things. There was no other explanation. Was there?

CHAPTER 18

The 5th of November finally came, clear and cold. As the time to leave for Arthur's Seat approached, I could barely contain my excitement. When my mum asked me to bring a box of woollen mittens down from storage, I didn't even complain, I was so happy.

I began climbing the ladder up to the attic. "Mittens? We haven't worn mittens in ages," I could hear Carl say.

"We wore them the last time we flew up to the top of the Jaggedy Peaks, don't you remember..." My mum's words became inaudible as I reached the top of the ladder and pushed open the hatch. I pulled myself up onto the floor above.

I hadn't been up here since that day I'd crashed off the roof (thanks, Carl). There were boxes and trunks everywhere, and everything was covered with a fine layer of dust. There was barely enough space to stand up, even without a pointy hat. I scanned the room, and soon found a box marked in my mum's spidery handwriting:

Winter Clothes

It was in the middle of a stack of three boxes, and I had to pull the box at the top down in order to get at it.

The box I heaved down was marked

Sparkler

Sparkler? That was the model of broom my parents had given Carl for his last birthday. The only reason I remembered was because the whole thing had ended up being *such* a big deal. My parents suddenly made Carl give it back without any explanation, other than to say it was "the wrong broom". Carl had loved that broom; it left a trail of sparks and coloured smoke as you flew, and looked really impressive. He was heartbroken when he had to give it back. My parents bought him another broom to replace it, but it wasn't the same. Whenever I tried to ask them about it, they changed the subject. So I stopped asking.

Why would there be a whole box devoted to a birthday present? My dad could be a bit of an anorak when it came to comparison shopping – maybe the box contained notes on other models and prices. Intrigued, I opened it.

It didn't contain my dad's nerdy comparison notes. Instead, there were dozens of file folders. I opened one, and saw that it was filled with several sheets of paper, each with a green-and-white photo attached. All of the photos showed a child, usually quite young – aged, I'd say, between about 150 and 500 years old. They all had some kind of injury – a broken arm, a broken leg – one was even wearing a neck brace. Why did Mum and Dad have these? And what did they have to do with the Sparkler, I wondered?

I closed the folder, and picked up another one beneath it. This second folder was bursting with lots of newspaper clippings; articles on yellowed parchment printed in green ink. I scanned the article on top quickly.

BROOM RECALLED

The popular broom model known as the 'Sparkler', manufactured by the Aerozoom Broom Corporation, has been recalled with immediate effect. Sources close to the company have revealed that the coloured smoke emitted by the broom at altitudes over 2 metres can be toxic.

There have been 56 incidents in which people riding the defective broom have been overcome by fumes and passed out, with many suffering from additional injuries as a result. Shares in the company have plummeted since the defect was discovered, but ABC's CEO was today unavailable for comment.

Defect? I couldn't believe it. So that explained why my parents had suddenly taken away Carl's new broom without explanation – the funny whirring noises! They weren't being mean; they were trying to protect him!

I leafed through the other articles. They basically all said different versions of the same thing: the Sparkler was dangerous. Forgetting the mittens, I scurried back to the hatch and climbed down the ladder. Breathless, I ran into the kitchen, where my parents were busy tidying up after dinner.

"Did you get the mittens, Slimeball?" Mum asked as she wiped down the counter top.

"Mittens?" I said absently. "Oh, the mittens... no."

My mum stopped in mid-wipe. "Ruby! I ask you for one thing—"

"I'll get them in a second," I said hurriedly. "Mum, Dad, I want to ask you something."

"What is it?" Mum said warily, in the tone of voice she uses when she thinks I'm going to ask for a fourth helping of lice pudding or a later bedtime.

"What's that box upstairs marked 'Sparkler'?"

My parents looked at each other, their eyes widening.

"Oh, nothing," Dad said hurriedly, rearranging the plates he had only just stacked. "Just a bunch of old photos."

"I know, I saw. But they're not of anyone we know."

Now my mum and dad looked really uncomfortable.

"And another thing," I said. "Why do you have all those newspaper clippings about the Sparkler?"

My dad gave me his 'I Am Not Amused' look. "What were you doing snooping through that box, young sorceress?"

"I was looking for the mittens, and it was in my way."

"Ruby, you can't go rifling through other people's things—" my mum began.

I interrupted her. No way was I going to be fobbed off this time. "Mum, Dad: *What is going on?*"

Dad put down the plates, and Mum set the sponge aside. "Sit down, kids."

Carl was pretending to be reading a comic book at the breakfast bar, but had obviously been eavesdropping (talk about snooping – I didn't see *him* getting into trouble). "Sure," he said eagerly, hopping off the stool and practically skipping over to the kitchen table. I don't know why he was so eager. The last time Mum and Dad had gathered us together like this our whole lives had changed. And not for the better.

When we were all sitting down, my mum began to speak. "Children," she said slowly, "there's something we haven't told you about the ABC, and why we left."

Carl and I looked at her expectantly. Finally, some answers!

My mum took a deep breath. "We didn't leave Hexadonia because we were made redundant. We were fired because we exposed corruption at the ABC, and frankly, we feared for our lives."

"Corruption?" said Carl quizzically. "What's that?"

"Very simply, it's when someone does something they know is wrong," said my dad.

"Like when I hide the TV remote so Ruby can't change the channel?" Carl asked.

"What? That was you? You little—" I aimed a nearby tea towel at his tiny head.

"Ruby!" my father snapped.

"No, it's bigger than that," Mum said. "It's when someone with a lot of responsibility, say a politician or the director of a company, does something they know is wrong."

"What kind of corruption?" I asked.

"Do you guys remember the whole Sparkler fiasco?" Dad asked.

"How could I forget?" Carl said bitterly.

"The broom was faulty. The smoke was making people faint and fall off."

"Oh," Carl said slowly, "is that why you took it away from me?"

Mum nodded. "But the company didn't want other parents to know about the problem, because then they'd demand their money back."

"You know your mum was in public relations," Dad explained. "It was her job to reassure the public that the broom was perfectly safe—"

"Basically, it was my job to lie," Mum continued.

"Is that what you're supposed to do in public relations?" Carl asked.

"Not really, no," Mum said. "But that's what they wanted me to do at the ABC."

"That's not very nice," Carl said quietly.

"No, it's not," my mum agreed. "Since Carl had a Sparkler, once I found out about all the problems with it, of course I was very concerned about his safety. And that got me thinking about all the other children who had that model too, and I felt I had to do something."

I couldn't believe it. My mum was a hero? I thought she spent most of her time cooking up her secret sauces and shooing Vronsky (in whatever form he happened to be in) off the furniture, but it turned out she had actually done something really cool.

"Your dad helped me gather information about all the incidents with the broom – we went around talking to people who had been affected – and then together we wrote a press release about the dangers."

"I bet that didn't go down well at work," I said.

"Well, no it didn't," Dad replied. "The company lost a huge amount of money, and its reputation was badly tarnished. In fact, not only did we both get fired, but the CEO of the ABC vowed to get revenge."

"On a tiny island," Mum added, "there's nowhere to hide. Moving from Hexadonia to one of the other islands in the Hexadonian Archipelago wouldn't be far enough, so we had no choice but to leave. We just didn't know what they might be capable of. We had to make sure you were both safe."

My mind was reeling. How could my parents have gone through all this without me knowing? I felt like an idiot, worrying about lost hats and school trips while they were dealing with this stuff.

"But look, kids," Dad said, brighter. "Our life here is pretty good, isn't it?"

"It's great!" Carl chirped. I could see he really meant it.

"Meh," I said, "I guess it's OK. But back home was better. Much better. Wasn't it?"

My mum looked up, but didn't say anything. My dad didn't say anything either.

"Wasn't it?" I said again. I couldn't believe my parents were voicing the very doubts that I was starting to have, not that I could let them know that. "I mean, of course we'd rather go back, wouldn't we?" I may have said this a bit too insistently.

Finally, my mum said slowly, "I don't know."

"What do you mean you don't know?"

"I mean, I don't know if I'd want to go back. Life isn't too bad here."

My dad pursed his lips, squinted, and cocked his head to one side, as though he were weighing something up. "It was hard at first, but things are going better now. We're settling in pretty well. Although we're not doing the same kind of jobs that we used to do, your mum and I have both been promoted at work, and my hair sculptures seem to have attracted something of a following, if I do say so myself."

It was true; I was beginning to see more and more people walking around Edinburgh with my dad's signature creations on their heads. They were pretty easy to spot.

"But life was so much better in Hexadonia!" I said. "We had magic, for one thing."

"Well, yes, the magic was good," my mum conceded. "But maybe not everything that went with it. Like working for the ABC, as it turned out."

I noticed that Carl had a pained expression on his face. It looked like he might be attempting to think. "They can't come after us, can they?" he asked.

My mum glanced quickly at my dad, and then said, "As long as we're here, we're perfectly safe. They don't know where we are. OK?"

"OK," Carl and I both said in unison.

I wondered, though, whether I should mention the three strange women I kept seeing. It seemed like too much of a coincidence that there was something so familiar about them, and that they seemed to keep popping up wherever I went. I was about to open my mouth, when my mum said abruptly, "Look, we can talk about this later. If we don't leave now we're going to be late. Come on. Everyone should wrap up warm. It's freezing tonight."

The moment had passed and I figured I was probably just being paranoid, so I ran back to the attic and got the mittens. We shrugged on coats (and Mum insisted on wearing her Burger Barn hat) and were out the door in under two minutes.

There was no way I was going to be late for this.

CHAPTER 19

As we sat on the busy bus down to Arthur's Seat, I reflected on everything I had just learned about why we'd left Hexadonia. Maybe going back there right now wasn't such a good idea. Maybe it would be better just to see if I could get my magic back and stay here, at least for the time being.

We got off the bus near the Parliament and walked the last few metres. Even though it was dark, I could see throngs of people climbing the hill. Everyone was wrapped up warm in big coats and hats and gloves. There was a full moon, and I could see the solid outline of Arthur's Seat against the inky night sky.

Dad scanned the crowds. He seemed a little on edge.

"All clear?" Mum asked.

Taking one last look around, my dad nodded. "I think so."

"Is *what* all clear?" I asked, but my dad had charged ahead, and didn't seem to hear me.

We walked up a grassy slope, passing a bonfire with people huddled round. A cheer went up as a life-size rag

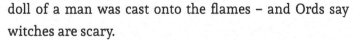

doll of a man was cast onto the flames – and Ords say witches are scary.

Carl pointed at two kids holding sticks sputtering colourful sparks. "Ooh! What are they? They look magic!"

"They're called sparklers, moron." I rolled my eyes.

"Ooh, like the broom?"

"Yes, like the broom. Seriously, sometimes I wonder if you—"

"That's enough, Ruby," my dad cut in. "We should get a good viewpoint. The fireworks will be starting soon." He looked at his wrist and frowned in confusion. "Where's my watch gone?"

"It's on the other wrist, Stan." This time it was my mum who rolled her eyes.

"Oh yes, of course." Dad shook his head.

I guess we know where I get my absent-mindedness from.

"I'll never get used to these infernal thingy-mabobs," he complained. "Nothing beats a good sundial."

The throngs of people thickened as we climbed the rocky path snaking up the hill. It was difficult to be sure of my footing in the dark, the path only lit by the surrounding crowd's sparklers and phone screens. I muttered the Snack Spell; even though I knew it wouldn't work, it was kind of meditative. I needed to calm my nerves; I was so excited I could hardly breathe. In a matter of minutes I might finally have my magic back!

As we continued climbing, I thought I caught a glimpse

of something very strange through the crowd. Even stranger than throwing model men full of newspaper on bonfires. The three women in massive woolly hats had turned up yet again, this time wearing funny patterned jumpers and those knee-length breeches that I'd seen people wearing when they played golf (I had watched a bit on TV with Dad and we hadn't been able to work out where the 'sport' part came in – it was basically just organised walking). They were all carrying golf bags filled with clubs. It was weird that they just happened to appear again, but even odder was the fact that there's no golf course on Arthur's Seat. What on earth were they doing? I squinted in the darkness, trying to get a closer look. Were those *broom* bristles poking out of one of their bags? Surely not. Wondering if I should go and investigate, the three women were suddenly swallowed by the crowd, and I lost them in the bustling sea of people.

"This looks like a good place," said my dad. He checked his watch, this time making sure he looked at the correct wrist. "The fireworks should be starting in a sec."

We had a fantastic view, with thousands of streetlights and bonfires below lighting up the night. This had to be the highest point in the city. Even my dad seemed to relax a bit, and dare I say it, actually seemed to be enjoying himself.

The fireworks began, and they were beautiful. They were like electric flowers, thousands of sparkling jewels raining down against the velvet black of the sky. I could barely contain my excitement. Everything was going to plan! After all this effort – convincing my parents to bring us here without them knowing why, struggling not to lose things for what seemed like ages, then having everything nearly go belly-up when I lost my hat – it had all been worth it.

I wondered again how this thing was actually going to work. Should I be looking out for a sign of some kind? Or would whoever was behind this send me another hext with instructions?

Just as I was about to sneakily check my phone, I was pulled out of my wandering thoughts by the sound of my mum shouting in alarm.

"No... it can't be," she gasped. "Stan, look!"

"What is it?" I said.

Both my parents were staring at something I couldn't see through the churning crowds. "How did they find us?" Dad said, his tone urgent.

My mother grabbed me and practically shook me. "Ruby! What made you bring us here?"

"I don't know what you mean," I lied.

"Ruby, why did you want to come here so badly? Who gave you the idea?"

I looked down. "I'm not supposed to say."

"Are you seriously choosing to listen to some stranger over your own parents?" my dad said incredulously. "I'm assuming it was a stranger who put you up to this?"

When he put it that way, I felt like an idiot. "I got this hext..." I began.

"You got a WHAT?" I've never seen my dad so angry. A vein at the side of his head began to pulse wildly.

"And when I replied, it—"

"You REPLIED to a hext from a STRANGER?" he shouted. People around us were beginning to stare.

"Even *I* know you're not supposed to do that," Carl said. "And I thought you were supposed to be older and wiser than me. How could you be so stupid?"

I can honestly say that I have never wanted to push my brother off an extinct volcano more than I did at that moment.

"We need to get out of here!" yelled Dad. "NOW!" He began looking around in panic, searching for a way through the surrounding crowds.

"But why?" I asked.

"It's the ABC," Mum said. "They've come for us! They've come to get their revenge!"

"But how—"

"I said NOW!" shouted my dad. He grabbed Carl's hand and pulled my mum by her elbow. I tried to follow, but someone in the crowd bumped into me in the darkness, momentarily blocking my path.

Suddenly, I heard something thud on the ground at my feet. I reached into my pocket, and realised that my phone had fallen out.

"Wait, I dropped something." I bent down to pick up

my mobile, fumbling for the heavy metal object in the darkness. When I stood up again, my family were already about 5 metres away, edging their way through the crowds.

"Ruby, hurry!" Mum called back. "Come on!"

I looked at my parents and brother pushing and stumbling towards the path, and then back to what had made them so frightened.

It turns out my witchy senses were right. The three 'golfers' I'd spotted earlier weren't avid sportswomen after all – they were witches, and they wanted revenge. As the fireworks exploded above them, a streak of light appeared to shoot directly towards the women, and they suddenly lit up. A powerful, fizzing energy surrounded them for a moment, and I smelled the familiar smokey tang of magic in the air. My dad's comments about fireworks rang in my head, too: *They make spells work here... Something about all the condensed energy in fireworks activates magic.*

Oh bats, were we in trouble.

Three pairs of glittering eyes focusing on my family, the witches cast off their golfing attire, robes darker than midnight spilling out from underneath. They threw their woolly headgear aside to reveal pointy hats, and from their club bags they pulled long, sleek combat brooms. No run-of-the-mill collapsible brooms for them. They obviously meant business. At that moment, a barrage of fireworks blotched the sky with colour, capturing the attention of the surrounding crowd.

My family barely had time to turn around before the

three witches were upon them, swooping down with their wands drawn. One of them, who had bright green hair that snaked in curly tendrils onto her shoulders, intoned:

This little chant will make you freeze
In such a way that no one sees.

I recognised that incantation. It was the Immobilising Invisibility Spell. Only witches with strong magic could perform it – the magic from the fireworks was obviously fuelling the witches' powers and making their spells even more potent. There were three purple flashes, and then my family disappeared. All that could be seen of them was a faint purple glow hovering above the grass on the mountainside.

I screamed, "Stay away from them!"

The witches dismounted. They had seen me, and were heading my way. "There she is," the very tall witch with an enormous brown wart on her nose said to her comrades. "The little greasy one. Now we can add her to the rest and do away with them once and for all."

The witch with small, gold-rimmed glasses addressed me directly. "So you thought you'd escape, girlie. That's hilariousssssss," she hissed. The others cackled.

"Let my family go!" I shouted.

"Oh, we'll let them go, all right," sniggered the tall one. "In fact, I'd say they'll be going quite far – down, that is – after we dump them in the sea."

I began to protest, but the curly-haired one cut me off. "Oh, don't worry about being lonely. You'll be joining them soon enough."

I had to act fast. I looked around me. The atmosphere was loud and chaotic on Arthur's Seat, and people were enjoying the fireworks, laughing and taking selfies, unaware that my family was in mortal danger. That gave me an idea. Looking round, I grabbed a selfie-stick out of the hands of a tourist couple, and raised it against the witch as though it were a sword. The couple gaped, but they were still holding their camera so they began to snap pictures of each other as I battled the witches in the background. They obviously thought it was some kind of impromptu theatre performance.

"Oh, that's how you want to play, is it?" the bespectacled one fixed her determined gaze on me. "OK, suit yourself." She held up her wand, ready to zap me.

But I was too fast. Lunging with my selfie-stick, I knocked her wand aside as a bolt of purple lightning flashed past my head, singeing my ear. The witch brought her wand back round, but I ducked and rained down a flurry of blows, not giving her time to ready her wand and utter a spell.

I thrust the stick into her cloak. She parried and, like a blowtorch, the white-hot tip of her wand cut through the pole I was holding. I was left with a smouldering, useless stump of plastic in my hand.

"Bludderfig," I groaned.

"You little grottlebud," the witch snarled, catching her breath and raising her wand. "Let's see how quick you are when you can't see!"

She muttered a spell:

Now do away with your sight,
Make it seem eternal night.

I lashed out with the remaining foot of the selfie-stick, knocking her wand just as she finished the incantation. It flashed brighter than any camera, right into her face. She threw off her glasses and clutched at her eyes, blinded by the sharp burst of light.

"I'm going to boil you in a vat of frog spawn!" the witch bellowed, staggering backwards. A couple of paces behind her was a 250-metre drop off the side of Arthur's Seat.

This really wasn't turning out to be a great day for her.

"I hope you have your broom handy," I remarked.

"My broom!" the witch cried, windmilling her arms frantically as she tried to catch her balance. But it was too late. She toppled over the cliff's edge, her furious howl growing quieter and quieter.

As I took a relieved breath, I heard the high-pitched whistle of speeding brooms heading towards me: the sound of witches on the warpath. I dodged several purple bolts of magic, each of which would have vaporised me if it had made contact.

Whirling round, I barely had time to drop to my

stomach as two brooms zoomed over my head, nearly grazing my back. I clambered to my feet. The pair of witches were swinging round in the air to attack again, so I dived into the nearest gorse bush. Pulling myself through the dark tangle of undergrowth, I ignored the thorny branches tearing and tugging at my clothes. At least here I'd be protected from the witches' brooms. Crawling on my hands and knees as fast as I could, I eventually emerged from the gorse onto the edge of a grassy clearance full of revellers.

I might only have seconds before they were upon me again so I needed to think fast. I frantically looked around for some kind of protection or weapon. To my amazement, scrabbling through the dark grass I found a stray firework amongst the litter. It was a red rocket. A few metres away, a man was trying to light a sparkler with a lighter, cupping his hand around it to shield it from the wind. I didn't think twice.

I scooped up the forgotten firework and bounded towards the man. Reaching out, I grabbed the lighter before he could do anything about it.

"Hey!" he cried.

"Sorry, life or death situation going on here," I explained, before examining my prize. I noticed that the man was already running away from me.

"Don't worry, I won't bite!" I called out, but he ignored me, picking up speed. "You'd think he'd seen a ghost," I muttered.

A croaky voice hissed behind me, "No. He's seen a WITCH."

I spun round, to be confronted by the curly-haired witch, her cloak flying behind her in the evening breeze. Slowly, she drew out her wand, levelling it at my chest. She was savouring every moment of this. Behind my back I discreetly flicked the lighter against the fuse of the firework. Dad had given Carl and me a long lecture about the dangers of fireworks before we'd left the house, but the witches were more dangerous than one firework. This was my only option. The rocket began to fizz.

"Nowhere to hide this time, eh?" the witch cackled. "We've been trailing you ever since you arrived in this Ord-infested place." She grimaced. "You were so pathetically easy to lure with that silly hext, it almost took the fun out of it. All we had to do was find a way to get you all here so we could use the energy of the fireworks to get rid of you for good."

Suddenly, though, her triumphant leer changed into a confused frown. "What's that you've got behind your back?"

"You want fireworks?" I asked. "Here, have mine!" I thrust the sparking, sputtering rocket into her billowing cloak.

And it went OFF.

I leaped backwards and dropped to the ground, shielding my eyes from the blinding glare. The witch screamed, colourful sparks cascading endlessly from her black robes. There was too much magic flowing into her, too fast.

"You little..." Her wand hand jerked in the air, randomly firing off red and purple bursts of light. Her shape became a shadow amongst a tornado of magic and fireworks.

BANG. BANG. BANG.

I pressed my face into the dirt, clamping my hands over my ears.

BANG. BANG.

One final, colossal explosion – a miniature supernova. And then...

Silence.

After a few mute seconds, I opened one eye a crack. A burned scrap of the witch's cloak floated into my view.

She was gone.

I had a vague recollection of my teacher back in Hexadonia – Mrs Zephyr – talking to us about magical combustion: *Now class, if your body ever happens to absorb too much magic in too short a space of time, it may... well... it may explode. Do NOT try this at home.*

Amazing as it was that I had just taken out not one, but *two*, evil witches, I didn't have time to dwell on the fact. I had to get back to my family before the last remaining witch got rid of them for good.

I hoped against hope that I wasn't too late.

CHAPTER 20

I scrambled back through the gorse bushes in the direction I'd come from, scratching and tearing what remained of my jacket. When I emerged, I looked around frantically for signs of my family. Fireworks were still exploding in the sky, and it was hard to make out specific shapes among the crowds. I started to panic. What if I never found them? What if the other witches had already dealt with them? They could be gone forever, and it was was all my fault. Desperate, I searched the ground where I was pretty sure we'd been standing.

Nothing.

Then, in the glow of the fireworks above, I spotted something papery crumpled up in the grass. It was a familiar orange-and-white colour. My mum's hat! Training my eyes a few metres up the hill, I thought I saw a very faint purple glow. I took a closer look, and YES – there they were! Or what was left of them, anyway.

As I approached the purple aura floating above the grass, I heard a raspy voice.

"There you are. How nice of you to make my job easier."

It was the tallest witch. I could see her sallow face and the huge brown wart on her nose, illuminated by the fireworks still exploding in the sky.

I tried to steady my voice. "You release my family right now!"

The witch cackled. "Oh? And who's going to make me?" She made a show of searching around for someone, as though she couldn't see me.

I was in a bit of a bind. Even if I defeated the witch, I wouldn't be able to release my family, because I didn't have any magic. The only way to save them was by getting the witch to release them herself. How on earth was I going to do that?

Suddenly, I had an idea. It was a long shot, but it was my only chance.

I had studied the Immobilising Invisibility Spell in school, and knew its UW, its Undoing Word. Every spell has a UW that can reverse its effects, but it only works if it's uttered by the witch who cast the spell. Knowing the UW wasn't much use to me at this point.

Unless...

"You can't do that to them," I announced. "There's been a law against using invisibility on foreign soil ever since the Treaty of Hexadonia in... uh... 964," I added, watching carefully to see how the witch would react.

She smirked. "You mean 963. What a moron!"

She was right. 963 was the crucial date that every

witch child learned in their very first history lesson. You didn't forget it; you just didn't.

"Y-yes," I pretended to stutter. "That's what I meant. 963. Yeah, that's it." I tried to look confused, using the expression Carl wore 80% of the time as inspiration. It seemed to work.

"Living among the Ords has messed with your mind," the witch sniggered. "You've become one of Them now, haven't you? You can't even remember the most basic facts about our history."

I couldn't believe my ears. Was she actually falling for it?

"Don't be ridiculous," I said. "Of course I can remember our history. Like, I can remember..." *How can I make her say the words?*, I thought frantically. My mind raced. Then suddenly, I had it.

"I can remember learning about the Great Dragon Rebellion of 1301. They dropped dragon tears over their enemies as they flew over the battlefield."

The witch threw her head back and cackled hysterically. "I can't believe the ignorance. Everyone knows they used dragon scales! Dragon's tears," she muttered, still laughing. "Ha! That's a good one!"

Bingo, as Ords like to say.

Dragon scales. She'd said it!

"That'll do nicely." I grinned, delighted that my plan had worked.

The witch paled, realising her mistake "No, wait—"

But it was too late. The purple glow hovering above

the ground disappeared, and I heard a loud popping sound. Looking over, I saw my family tumble onto the grass.

"Are you OK?" I cried.

"Yes!" my dad shouted. "Ruby! We have to get out of here!" He helped my mum to her feet and grabbed Carl by the hand.

"I'm sorry, Dad," I said, shaking my head. "Just one more to go."

"You listen to me!" he shouted. "We've got to—"

"That's ENOUGH!" I bellowed.

I'd always wanted to say that. You know how they say girls end up becoming their mothers? Well, for just a brief moment, I had become my dad.

"Sorry Dad, Mum, I'll see you back home. I have some unfinished business to attend to." I couldn't let this last witch get away, I just couldn't.

My dad ran over and reached out to take hold of my elbow, just as the last witch was speeding past me. I eluded his grasp and grabbed onto the end of the broom. The witch veered upwards, leaving me hanging by one hand.

"RUBY!" my mum yelled. "Come back!"

As the witch took me higher and higher, I saw my family grow smaller and smaller. They looked like tiny insects crawling down the hill.

Dangling dangerously, it was only then that I second-guessed what I had done. Maybe it wasn't so clever.

"Put me down!" I shouted.

"Oh I will, just you wait... " the witch growled from atop the broom. "No one, I mean *no one*, kills my pals and gets away with it. You've shot right to the top of my 'To Do' list. I'll deal with you first, and go back for the family."

We climbed further into the night sky until we were above the exploding fireworks. The smell of smoke filled my nostrils. I hadn't flown since we left Hexadonia, and I wished I could have enjoyed the experience. I couldn't, though, because I was so terrified. There's a difference between *flying* a broom and *clinging on* to one for dear life. The hand supporting my weight was starting to hurt, and it was growing slippery with sweat. I didn't dare try to swing my other hand up in case I destabilised the whole thing.

We soon levelled off, and began heading north. Edinburgh flashed by beneath me: the New Town, the Botanic Gardens, then the Leith docks, where I had arrived with my family what seemed like a million years ago. So much had happened since then. Thinking about my mum and dad, and even Carl, made me feel a little stronger. They had done so much to make sure we were safe, now it was my turn. The broomstick suddenly quivered to a halt a few hundred metres above the Firth of Forth. My hand was really hurting now. I wasn't sure how much longer I could hang on.

The witch peered down at me as I dangled helplessly from the broom. Grinning, she leaned over and peeled away one of my fingers. "This little piggy went to market," she cackled madly. Her eyes glowed orange.

Now I was hanging by just four fingers.

"How about a swim?" the witch said. "A little midnight dip. How about that?"

My hand felt like it was on fire. Slowly but surely, it was slipping.

"This little piggy stayed home." The witch pried another finger off the broom.

Three fingers.

"And after you've had a nice refreshing paddle, I'm going to take care of your family. For good," the witch hissed. "We've waited so patiently to get you all, Ruby, so patiently. Tonight couldn't come soon enough."

"B-but why follow us here?" I stuttered. My heartbeat was out of control as I glanced down at the dark, liquid depths below. "My mum and dad were only trying to help when they let everyone know about the Sparkler. They saved kids' lives."

"Your parents inflicted a lot of damage on the Aerozoom Broom Corporation. We lost millions of ingots and the shareholders were furious. The CEO couldn't have that, could he? Mummy and Daddy should have left well alone. Now you'll all pay the price. Might as well start with you. Goodbye, Ruby," she smirked. "Enjoy your swim!"

The witch peeled off another finger, and I couldn't hold on any longer. My hand slid from the polished wood of the broom, and I fell.

CHAPTER 21

I looked down at the black water whizzing up to meet me, faintly illuminated by the moonlight. So this was it. I knew I was right to be afraid of water, I knew it. I closed my eyes, waiting for the end.

Seconds later I felt something envelop me. If it was water, it wasn't as cold as I thought it would be. And not as horrible, either. In fact, not horrible at all.

Confused, I cracked open one eye.

I wasn't dead. I wasn't even wet.

Instead, I was in the talons of a massive bird, gliding a few metres above the freezing water. The bird appeared to be a gigantic osprey. It purred contentedly.

Hang on, *purred*?

"Vronsky?" I cried. The bird purred again in affirmation.

The witch hovered on her broom a few metres away, snarling. She wasn't going to let me go. As Vronsky flapped his enormous wings, I felt a whirlwind of emotions rush through me. I was afraid, but I knew that I couldn't let him carry me away – the witch would come back for my family, and I had no doubt she'd finish them off next time.

I saw her adjust the position of her broom and pick up speed. She was heading straight towards me.

I had to do something. But what? I didn't have any weapons, and I definitely didn't have any magic. Vronsky had saved my life, but I couldn't see how he could help me defeat the witch. Maybe if I had something I could throw at her...

Then I remembered. I did have something I could use, something heavy. But it was my one link to home.

The witch was so close now that I could see her contorted face twisted into a determined grimace, and I could smell her mildewy breath. I thought about the fear on my family's faces as I'd climbed higher and higher on the broom.

I made a decision.

I wasn't voted Most Valuable Player in the Hexadonian Cockroach League for nothing. I pulled the heavy, lead-and-bronze-encased phone out of my pocket, took one last look at it for memory's sake, and lobbed it towards the witch. It hit her left shoulder soundly, causing her to lose her balance, just for a second. But a second was all it took. She plummeted like a boulder, too surprised to utter any spell or incantation to save herself. I heard a thunderous **SPLASH** in the darkness below.

I couldn't believe it. I had actually done it. I had defeated all three witches. My family were finally safe. My mind was racing as Vronsky swooped down to land and gently deposited me on my feet at the water's edge.

"Vronsky, you're a life saver!" I hugged him tight. But that didn't even begin to express how grateful I was to him.

Vronsky purred again and swished his tail feathers happily.

I slowly sank down to my knees on the rocky beach. I could barely get my head round what had just happened. I had been so excited about that hext, and the prospect of getting my magic back, that I had overlooked all the warning signs that it was a trick. How could I be so *stupid*? The thought of the risk I had exposed my family to made me feel sick. I put my head in my hands and uttered the Snack Spell to calm down, and then I uttered it again, and again once more for good measure. Something about saying the familiar words made me feel better.

When I finally lifted my head, I saw something unbelievable. Something so completely unexpected that it took me a minute to realise what was happening.

A snack appeared on a large rock in front of me. Actually, not one snack, but three: a dish of candied gnats, a plate of fried earthworms, and a glass of bat's milk. Maybe I was so traumatised I was actually hallucinating?

Leaping up, I cautiously went to touch the fried earthworms. But instead of my fingers passing straight through them, I felt their crispy coating in all its greasy goodness. They were real! Without a second thought, I quickly wolfed down the delicacies. Battling evil witches was hungry work.

When I had polished off the whole lot, though, a thought occurred to me. The appearance of this yummy food could only mean one thing.

<u>I HAD MY MAGIC BACK!</u>

I screamed.

I screamed so loud it startled Vronsky. His feathers sprung out on end and he hissed in alarm.

"It's OK, Vronsk," I smoothed them back down, "I've got my magic back!"

Whooping with joy, I tried to pick him up and swing him round, but he was just too big.

I had got my magic back. I couldn't believe it. But how? The hext had been a trick. And then I remembered: when you defeat a witch in battle, you get an act of magic in return (that's in the Treaty of Hexadonia too). So, not only had my magic returned, but it was for the best possible reason: because I had defeated the evil witches. Nothing like having to earn it to make you appreciate the value of magic, that's for sure. I gleefully imagined all the magic I was going to do. *Where to begin, where to begin?*

After much deliberation, I finally settled on the Conjuring Spell. Vronsky and I needed to get home, and I wasn't sure how long his osprey form might last, so I decided to summon a broom. Might as well be practical.

> When it's time to zip and zoom,
> Let's conjure up a speedy broom.

But nothing happened. No broom. I scratched my head. It had been a while since I'd actually performed magic; I figured I must be rusty. I tried again.

When it's time to zip and zoom,
Let's conjure up a speedy broom.

Still nothing. Could I be misremembering the spell? Or could the spell be somehow faulty?

I looked over at Vronsky, who was trying to groom his wings. I uttered the Snack Spell again, just as a test:

Eye of newt and hoof of yak
Let's conjure up a tasty snack.

Nothing. Not a thing.

Hang on. When you defeat a witch, you get *one* act of magic. Just one.

I had defeated *three* witches, so I had earned *three* acts of magic. Sounds great, right?

But here's the thing. I had blown all three of them by saying the Snack Spell three times to calm down.

THE SNACK SPELL.

How did this happen?? It's like that fairy tale where the guy is given two wishes and he gets into an argument with his wife and in anger shouts that he wishes she had a sausage for a nose. He gets his wish, but then he has to use his second wish to change the sausage back into a nose again. Nightmare. Let's just say I understood how he felt.

I sat on the rock and buried my head in my hands again. How could I be such a complete bludderfig?

But as I thought more about what had just happened, I began to feel a little less awful. For one (or three) glorious moments, I had my magic back again. Hadn't that been what I wanted all along? Plus, snacks are nothing to sneeze at. It may not have been the whole enchilada (so to speak), but maybe it was enough. For now, anyway.

I was so absorbed in my thoughts that it took me a minute to realise that a large, pointed beak was tapping me on the shoulder. I looked up. Vronsky was standing next to me, flapping his wings impatiently and hopping from talon to talon.

"What?"

He flapped more insistently and turned his head skyward.

"You think we should go somewhere?"

More flapping. I took that as a 'yes'.

"Where, Vronsk? Home? You think we should go home?"

Vronsky flapped his wings so hard he lifted off the ground a few metres.

"Yeah," I said, the weariness of the day's events finally catching up with me. I figured Mum, Dad and Carl would head there eventually too. "You're right. Let's go home."

And with that, he gently grasped me in his claws and we soared into the night.

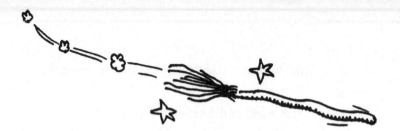

CHAPTER 22

"Ruby, if you don't get up *this second* I'm throwing your Weetabix in the bin!"

I opened my eyes. Nope; *still* not a morning person.

I wriggled out of my dragon-skin duvet, dragged myself out of bed, hurriedly washed and dressed, and staggered down the stairs to breakfast. Mum, Dad and Carl were all seated at the table.

"So glad you could join us," my dad said.

"Uh-huh," I mumbled.

"You're looking bright-eyed this morning," my mum observed.

I grunted.

Vronsky, who had turned back into a cat the evening before, jumped up into my lap and began purring. I scratched him behind the ears. It was so nice to hear an actual cat purring again. Though his osprey form had been convenient for quickly popping to the shops and back – oh, and rescuing me from evil witches.

"Now, Ruby, before you go to school," my dad said,

"there are a few things we need to discuss. For one thing, this business of hexting with strangers..."

Mercifully, before he could get any further into his well-prepared lecture, the doorbell rang.

Carl leaped up to open it, but I shoved past him in the hall and got there first.

It was Georgia and Logan, collecting us to walk to school. They had turned up one morning a week or so ago and it had just become a regular thing. It wasn't as fun as riding a broomstick to school, but I had to admit it was nice to have found a real friend in Georgia.

"Hi, Ruby. Lovely morning!" Logan chirruped from the doorstep. His school backpack was almost bigger than he was.

Georgia looked down at her little brother and rolled her eyes. "You are *so* weird."

She shook her head and gave me a despairing look that seemed to say, *Brothers!*.

"Can't stop to chat now, Dad." I grabbed my backpack and ran out the door, pulling Carl behind me.

"But wait—"

"Gotta run. Catch you later!" I called out. We turned onto the path and set off towards school.

As we walked up the street, I reflected on everything that had happened on Bonfire Night. Even though my parents still gave me a hard time about stuff, I think the fact that I saved them from the evil clutches of the Aerozoom Broom Corporation's henchwomen had earned me a lot of brownie points, at least for the time being.

I was a little upset, though, about wasting my precious magic on the Snack Spell, of all things. I couldn't help thinking about all the other spells I could have cast, all the other magical deeds I could have done…

But thinking like that wasn't going to get me anywhere. The important thing was that I had got my magic back, even if it was only briefly, and even if it wasn't my first choice of spell.

The point is, I did it.

And if I did it once, then maybe – OK, it's a long shot, but you never know – just maybe, I can do it again.

RUBY McCRACKEN'S GUIDE TO THE ORDINARY WORLD

INTRODUCTION

Are you planning a visit to the Ordinary World? I don't know why you would, it's awful here, but hey, maybe you like the idea of a place with no magic, no decent food and nothing interesting to do...

Anyway, the Ord World can be strange to us Hexadonians, so I've written this guide to help you navigate some of the strange Ord customs. Enjoy!

First Things First

☆ Magic doesn't work in the Ord World. Not even the Snack Spell.

☆ Don't forget to convert your cash to Ord money. You'll get some funny looks if you try to pay with bronze ingots.

☆ Familiars react strangely to the Ord World. Be prepared for some minor shapeshifting...

EATING AND DRINKING

✭ When going to a restaurant in the Ordinary World, ask WHAT'S on the menu, not WHO.

✭ Ords eat eggs from chickens instead of spiders, and their milk comes from cows instead of bats!

✭ Ords actually LIKE chocolate, and ice cream. Disgusting!

✭ They don't have sandwitches in the Ord World. They have something similar called sandwiches, but they have the filling on the inside, which just doesn't make sense.

ENTERTAINMENT

✮ A Spelling Bee in the Ord World doesn't actually involve any magic spells. Instead, they just have to say the letters of a word in the right order. So boring.

✮ Don't expect to find live snakes in any Ord World board games. Their version of Snakes and Ladders is just pictures on a board. This place is so incredibly dull.

✮ Apparently, an orange head impaled on a stick is not an appropriate craft activity for Girl Guides.

FASHION

☆ Ords have something called lipstick, which is like our lobestick but instead of putting it on their earlobes, they put it on — you guessed it — their lips. I mean — I can't even...

☆ Hats aren't allowed in the classroom — unless you tell your teacher you have a highly infectious disease.

☆ Ords actually try to prevent their teeth from rotting and falling out. They go to see someone called a "dentist" who makes their teeth white and clean. Urgh!

Making Friends
With Ords

☆ Flowers are thought to be a good thing. Ords actually like them, and give them to each other as gifts (and they heartlessly kill weeds, if you can believe it).

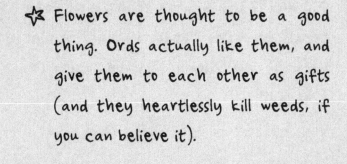

☆ Loads of people in the Ord World are scared of really normal things like spiders, ghosts, vampires and even witches!

☆ Instead of normal nicknames like "Slimeball", people call you "Honey". Which is weird because as we all know, honey is something criminals are forced to eat in prison.

I hope your visit to the Ord World is more fun, less permanent, and less dangerous than mine!

Oh, and if you wanted to bring me some treats from the Outdoor Insect Market back in Hexadonia, I'd be eternally grateful!